He'd never for...

But now he had to w...

After he cleaned the cut on her hand, he handed her a roll of gauze with his prosthetic hand, making sure to keep his distance.

"You'll have to hold it in place while I wrap," Becca said.

He noted the irony in the situation. They were both handicapped now.

Joe held the gauze against her skin, refusing to consider how long it had been since he'd touched her. A lifetime ago. But the memories were as vivid now as then.

When she finished and raised her head, their eyes met…and she froze. He stepped back but she stopped him.

"Joe." She said it softly, barely a whisper as it slid over him. "I'm so sorry." Her eyes pleaded with him.

Sorry? She was twelve years too late for sorry. As he turned and walked out of the barn, his head cautioned him. *Don't make the same mis...*

So ...

Tina Radcliffe has been dreaming and scribbling for years. Originally from Western New York, she left home for a tour of duty with the Army Security Agency stationed in Augsburg, Germany, and ended up in Tulsa, Oklahoma. Her past careers include certified oncology RN and library cataloger. She recently moved from Denver, Colorado, to the Phoenix, Arizona, area, where she writes heartwarming and fun inspirational romance.

Books by Tina Radcliffe

Love Inspired

The Rancher's Reunion
Oklahoma Reunion
Mending the Doctor's Heart
Stranded with the Rancher
Safe in the Fireman's Arms
Rocky Mountain Reunion
Rocky Mountain Cowboy

Rocky Mountain Cowboy

Tina Radcliffe

Recycling programs
for this product may
not exist in your area.

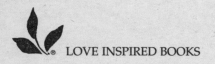

LOVE INSPIRED BOOKS

ISBN-13: 978-0-373-62253-5

Rocky Mountain Cowboy

Copyright © 2016 by Tina M. Radcliffe

www.Harlequin.com

Printed in U.S.A.

Do not remember the former things, nor consider the things of old. Behold, I will do a new thing, now it shall spring forth; shall you not know it? I will even make a road in the wilderness and rivers in the desert.
—*Isaiah* 43:18–19

This book is dedicated to the heroes in my life,
my husband, Tom, and my dad, Joe.

Acknowledgments

Many thanks to beta readers Nancy Connally
and Vince Mooney. They took the time to
help me saddle the horse and get this story
off on the right path.

Thank you to the people who assisted me
with the research on this story.
All errors are wholly mine.

To real-life Nebraska rancher Ivan Connealy
and his author wife, Mary Connealy, thank you
for your time, insights and information on cattle
and hay. Thanks to Missy Tippens
for that calf-roping assistance!

Thank you to Rob Dodson, CPO, FAAOP clinical
manager with Advanced Arm Dynamics, who
connected me with the amazing Barry Landry.
Barry is a transradial amputee who utilizes
the Michelangelo myoelectric prosthesis and
happens to be an amateur rodeo cowboy. Not
only does Barry ride horses, but he ropes cattle.
Thank you, Barry, for taking time to answer
all my questions. You can find out more about
Advanced Arm Dynamics and the Michelangelo
at www.armdynamics.com.

A final thank-you to my editor, Giselle Regus,
for her endless patience with a slow writer,
and insightful editing on this book.

Chapter One

It had been a good many years since Rebecca Anshaw Simpson had inhaled the earthy combination of cattle, horse and hay that was home. As the scents wove their way in through the vents of her car, it seemed like only yesterday that she was a kid, riding like a swift rush of wind through the valley of Paradise, Colorado. Life was simple then. So blessedly simple.

Rebecca yawned and rolled down her window to fully appreciate the enticing perfume of home. As she stretched, her aching neck protested. The muscles were stiff because she'd fallen asleep inside the ancient compact Honda.

When an almost icy spring breeze moved through the car, Rebecca pulled her down-filled vest closer.

A horse and rider appeared in the distance. Silhouetted against the horizon and the rising sun's orange glow, the man in the dark Stetson approached at a rapid clip, with two dogs racing alongside.

She'd know that profile anywhere.

Joe Gallagher.

Tension crept along her shoulders. She'd had serious reservations about taking this job because of Joe. They'd dated all through high school, even though she was two years younger than him. Joe was her first love. Until she'd dumped him.

Young and naive, she'd been swept off her feet at the end of her sophomore year of college, and eloped with Nick Simpson.

What a trusting fool she'd been. For a lingering moment, Rebecca allowed herself to contemplate what life would have been like if she'd stuck with the homeboy.

"It doesn't matter," she whispered.

None of it did. All that mattered was today. Life as she'd known it had been stolen from her two years ago. She had returned to Paradise to begin again.

What irony that she should be returning home to the man she had scorned. Forced to face him again, after so many years. The Lord surely had a sense of humor opening the door to this assignment. OrthoBorne Technology had not only given her a job, but it had dangled a huge bonus, like a proverbial carrot on a stick. She'd taken the bait and was determined to make the most of this chance.

When the man on the horse was close enough for her to see his midnight-black hair peeking out from under his hat and the shadow of a beard on his face, Rebecca inhaled a sharp breath. Joe Gallagher had changed. He'd become ruggedly handsome in the years since they'd parted.

"Becca?" Joe slid off his horse and approached the gate. His deep voice reflected stunned surprise, and the underlying tone was anything but welcoming.

Tired of craning her neck, she opened the car door and stepped out, stretching her stiff legs while discreetly pulling down the sleeves of her sweater. She still had to look up to meet his gaze. Joe was taller than she remembered, with that same dangerous loner aura.

He rested his gloved left hand on the top of the gate,

while his other hand, the prosthetic one, according to her notes, remained tucked away inside the pocket of his fleece-lined denim jacket. For a long minute he simply stared. It was as though he was looking through her, to the past.

The lean black-and-white cattle dogs at his feet barked and raced in energetic circles, eager to be part of the conversation.

"Sit," Joe commanded, his voice steely.

The animals instantly obeyed.

"Been a long time," he finally said, his gaze returning to hers.

Rebecca tried to gauge what he was thinking, but his expression was unreadable. Apparently he still held everything deep inside.

"It has been, hasn't it? A very long time," she murmured. "I heard you joined the army after college."

"Yeah. When my dad died, I went ahead and took an early discharge."

"I'm so sorry about your father," she said, immediately regretting her words. "I, um, I know how close you two were."

He gave a quick nod of acknowledgment. "What about you?" he asked. "Home for a visit? Is your husband with you?"

At Joe's question, everything around Rebecca slowed down and began to blur. The world came to a stunning halt as the words slipped from her mouth.

"Nick is dead."

Joe jerked back slightly, eyes widening a fraction. "I didn't know. I'm sorry for your loss."

Unmoving, she stared at him. The surprise on his face seemed genuine enough. Could Joe Gallagher be the only person in Paradise, in Colorado for that matter, who didn't know about the accident? The trial? Hadn't it been splashed in every newspaper? The grandson of one of the founding families of Paradise Valley had been taken from this world far too soon.

Apparently Joe didn't know her life had been on hold for the last twenty-four months as she awaited the results of the jury trial.

"You okay?" Joe asked when she didn't answer.

"Yes. Yes. Sorry." Rebecca leaned against the Honda and massaged her arm. Glancing down, she realized what she was doing and stopped. "Long drive from Denver. I started out Friday afternoon. It was so late that I just slept in the car."

His eyes rounded. "You spent the night in your car? Why didn't you drive to your mom's house?"

"No. That's not what I meant. I didn't spend the night in the car. Two hours. A nap."

Joe raised a brow.

Rebecca shrugged. "There was a huge accident on I-25 outside the Springs, and then I ran into issues with the starter when I hit Alamosa."

"Why are you parked here?"

She nodded to the sign on the gate. "I thought this was still the main entrance to the ranch. Until I saw the sign."

Joe grimaced as he, too, glanced at the sign.

"Do not cross this pasture unless you can do it in nine seconds, because the bull can do it in ten. Please close the gate."

"That would be my mother's handiwork."

"Why not put a padlock on the gate?"

"It's the ingress for emergency vehicles. If I put a padlock on it, then I have to remember where the key is." He paused and looked at her, eyes narrowed. "Wait a minute. Why are you at Gallagher Ranch?"

"Since I have to drive out here to see you anyhow, I thought I'd do a dry run. By the time I finally arrived, I was a little more tired than I realized." She lifted a hand. "Thus the nap."

"Whoa. Whoa. Whoa." When he suddenly straightened and raised a hand, the black horse behind him whinnied and stepped back several paces, causing the dogs to bark.

Joe laid a comforting hand on the animal and silenced the dogs again. "Let's start over here. Did you say you're here to see me?"

Rebecca glanced at her watch. "Yes. Our meeting is scheduled for Monday morning."

"Things have been pretty hectic around here, but I don't forget appointments. And I'm even less likely to have forgotten an appointment with..."

Rebecca swallowed when his words trailed off. What had he been about to say? With someone who had treated him so callously? The girl who dumped him.

Joe pulled the glove off his right hand and then tugged the matching one off his left hand using his teeth, before taking out his phone. The skin tone silicone cover of the myoelectric prosthesis made his right hand appear nearly identical to his left. She couldn't help assess that he really didn't use the prosthesis, apparently utilizing the device simply as a placeholder.

After fiddling with the phone for a moment, he paused and slowly met her gaze. Complete shock was reflected in his eyes. "Are you..."

"I'm the therapist who's been assigned to complete the certification for your prosthesis."

"You're a therapist?"

She nodded.

"I thought they were sending someone from Denver.

They told me it was someone who would help with those media people who are coming, as well."

His voice was edged with irritation, and Rebecca held her breath and stepped back from him.

"They are. They did. I am."

Joe Gallagher's face looked like he'd just been struck with a cattle prod.

She crossed her arms and stated the obvious. "This is going to be a problem."

He took off his Stetson and then slapped it back on so that it rested at the back of his head, revealing more of his jet-black hair. She could clearly see that his moss-green eyes were troubled.

"Joe?"

"I guess it better not be, because the way I see things, I don't have much choice. Do I?"

"You tell me." She looked him straight in the eye. "Is our history going to get in the way?"

"History? Is that the politically correct term these days?" He offered a bitter chuckle.

She studied him once again. His face was a mask, his gaze shuttered.

"No, Becca," he finally continued. "You don't have to worry. Even this Colorado cowboy realizes that was a long time ago. We were kids. This is business. More important, the future of Gallagher Ranch depends on me completing the requirements of my contract with Ortho-Borne. I cut a deal to pay off this fourteen-karat-gold myoelectric arm." His eyes pinned her. "And I always keep my word."

Joe turned his head to glance out at the land, and she realized she'd been dismissed. The knowledge burned.

"So Monday, then?" she asked quietly.

"That's fine. I'm past the main house. A bit farther up the road. Two-story log cabin."

She nodded.

He turned to her. "When do your friends arrive?"

"They aren't my friends." Rebecca bristled. "I don't even know who was contracted for this job, except that there's a videographer and a copywriter."

"When will they finish?"

"That is wholly dependent upon you and the weather."

He offered a slow shake of his head that said her answer wasn't nearly satisfactory enough. "What about certification? How long do you think that will take?"

"Once again, everything depends on you. I don't anticipate more than four weeks reviewing your ADLs."

He straightened, jaw tense, and his face was almost thunderous. "Four weeks! Four weeks? I have a ranch to run."

"Joe, that's exactly why it will take that long. In fact, knowing how a ranch runs, I asked for extra time so our sessions don't interfere with what you have to do at the ranch or with the media crew."

"And what's an ADL?"

"Activities of daily living."

He sucked in a breath but said nothing.

"Look, that doesn't mean we can't get everything done earlier than scheduled. I'll accompany you on your routine chores, schedule one-on-one sessions related to your ranch work. Then I'll assist you to incorporate the prosthesis into your daily life that isn't ranch related."

"Can you still ride?"

"What?" She shook her head, certain she'd heard the terse question incorrectly.

"Ride. Do you ride?"

Rebecca frowned. "I was born in a saddle, like you were. Cowgirls don't forget how to ride."

The tension in Joe's shoulders eased a bit. "That'll help, because, no offense, Becca, but I plan to graduate way ahead of schedule."

"While it's my job to treat you the same as all my clients, there is no doubt in my mind that you'll beat all records getting this done. Then I'll be gone, and you can go back to your life."

Rebecca looked up at him, standing tall and proud, profiled against the land. For a brief moment she imagined she saw a glimpse of something familiar from years ago and the closeness they once shared.

That was crazy because yesterday was long gone. Once again Rebecca reminded herself that it was high time to start looking forward instead of behind.

"I'm sorry, Mrs. Simpson, but it's no longer available."

"How can that be? I called before I left Denver to make sure everything was set."

Joe turned at the sound of Becca's voice.

He'd sidestepped the woman for twelve years, and now he managed to run into her twice in the space of a few hours?

She stood on the sidewalk of downtown Paradise, and was obviously doing her best to get her point across to a wiry guy as they stood outside the real-estate office.

How little the years had changed her. He'd been stunned to see her at the fence this morning. The years had tumbled back, and he realized with painful clarity that the tall, lean beauty who'd stolen his heart at sixteen apparently could still tie him in knots.

The difference was that this time he had a strong rope

anchored to his heart, holding down those once generous emotions of his. *Only a fool gets burned twice.*

He'd made more than his share of mistakes in his life, and he liked to believe he'd learned from every single one of them. Joe glanced down at his prosthesis, remembering the farm accident that had taken his limb. He pushed the memory away and focused on the here and now.

Joe glanced back down the street. From a distance, he could feel the tension in the air. He tucked himself back into the doorway of a shop, grateful he stood well behind Becca's line of sight.

She pushed strands of dark hair away from her face as she dug in her purse to pull out neatly folded papers. "You took my deposit and my credit-card information. Why, you even mailed me a receipt. I have the paperwork right here."

Confusion laced Becca's voice. To her credit, she maintained her composure, though her hands were clenched tightly around her purse.

The Realtor adjusted his tie, swallowed and shrugged, obviously avoiding eye contact with her. "I've reversed the charges, ma'am. No worries."

"No worries?" She blinked and began to gesture with her hands. "No worries?"

Joe found himself unable to resist listening to the conversation, and at the same time fighting the urge to come to her defense. Why should he? Becca had made it clear a long time ago that she didn't want him in her life. No, he reminded himself, her return to Paradise and whatever was going on here was none of his business.

"Are you kidding me?" Becca continued, her voice louder and tight with frustration. "Couldn't you go inside and check your files again?"

"No need," the man returned, his voice low and upbeat in an effort to defuse the situation. "That's why I stepped outside. I saw you coming, and I thought I'd save you some time."

"Okay, so if that rental isn't available, do you mind telling me what is?"

"Ma'am, I don't have anything for you right at the moment. Maybe you could try some of those new condos down by Paradise Lake."

"I can't afford those."

"I'm real sorry, Mrs. Simpson. It's just one of those things."

"One of *what* things?"

The young man squirmed while gesturing helplessly.

"Look, I rented the house a month ago. Not only that, but your ad today in the *Paradise Gazette* says you have at least five summer rentals still available in the area. Now you're claiming that you have none?"

"Ma'am, I'm real sorry."

Shoulders slumped, Becca shook her head. "This is unbelievable," she murmured.

An ache he couldn't explain gnawed at Joe. Without thinking, he strode down the sidewalk, zigzagging around people, oblivious to a sudden flurry of shoppers creating obstacles in his path, and stepped up to Becca and the real-estate agent.

"Everything okay here, Becca?"

Startled, her brown eyes popped open and she looked up at him. "I... I have this under control, Joe."

"Doesn't sound like it to me," he returned, purposely shooting the other man a scowl.

"*Joe.*"

He met Becca's gaze.

"You need to stay out of this. Besides, my business

is done here." She turned on her heel and walked away, her face shielded by a curtain of chocolate-brown waves.

Behind him, Joe heard the sound of bells as the real-estate agent disappeared into the storefront.

Joe quickly yanked open the door, setting the bells into a wicked frenzy. The guy behind the desk had a solicitous smile on his face when he turned around.

Then he saw Joe.

He straightened and inched back farther behind the desk. "May I help you?"

"I sure hope so..." Joe glanced at the man's name tag. "Jason."

Jason came out from behind the desk and thrust a hand in greeting. Apparently his plan was to pretend that the incident outside moments before had never happened. "Have we met?" he asked.

"No, we haven't. Joe Gallagher. Gallagher Ranch." Joe looked the other man up and down before offering his prosthetic hand.

Jason's eyes widened, and he dropped his own hand.

"New to town?" Joe asked.

"Yes, I am. How may I help you, sir?"

"I want to rent a house."

"I'm sure we can fix you up. Anything in particular you're looking for?"

"I'd like the one that you were supposed to lease to Rebecca Simpson."

Jason's face paled and he stepped backward, once again effectively putting the desk between him and Joe. "Sir, I don't recommend that you get involved in that situation." Tiny beads of perspiration popped out along his upper lip.

"What situation is that, Jason?"

The man swallowed hard before darting to the front

door and switching the sign from Open to Closed. "Sir, if you'll excuse me, I'm closed for the day."

Joe followed him, getting squarely in the man's personal space, towering over him with as much intimidation as he could muster. "Off the record, Jason, tell me what's going on."

Jason swallowed again as if he was desperate for a glass of water and a way to get rid of Joe.

"Can you tell me why you just turned down a paying customer?"

"I… I…"

Joe shook his head and growled, "I don't like this, Jason."

"I don't much like it either, but I have a wife and a new baby to think about."

Joe turned on his boot heel and left the office. Though he did his best not to slam the door, the bells were once again ringing a dissonant tune behind him as he put distance between himself and a sour situation.

It was time for a little chat with the sheriff of Paradise. Joe started toward his truck and then changed his mind. Walking was just what he needed. He headed in the other direction, cutting through the park in the center of town and past the gazebo toward the office of Sam Lawson, where he pulled open the heavy wooden door.

This wasn't about Becca, he reassured himself. It was the principle of the thing. No one should be treated unfairly. Especially in Paradise.

Bitsy Harmony MacLaughlin, the administrative assistant, sat at a huge battered desk, guarding the entrance to Sam's office like a geriatric bouncer.

"Sam available?" he asked.

Bitsy stood and realigned the silver braided knot on

the top of her head. "The sheriff is on the phone. Give him five minutes."

Joe nodded. He wasn't eager to lose the momentum of his purpose by chitchatting with Bitsy, so he turned to examine the bulletin board.

"Cup of coffee, Joe? It's fresh."

He eyed the pot and sniffed the air. "What do you have brewing?"

"Vanilla caramel pecan."

He did his best not to grimace. "Um, no. I'm going to pass. Thank you very much, ma'am."

Bitsy poured herself a mugful from the carafe, all the while shooting him inquisitive glances. "I heard you've got some Hollywood people coming out to your ranch next week to film a movie."

His eyes widened with surprise. "Hollywood? A movie? Where did you hear that?"

"Here and there."

Joe met her gaze. "I never told anyone they were coming."

"They did." Bitsy's blue eyes were unwavering. "Made reservations at the Paradise Bed and Breakfast and chatted with the clerk. She mentioned it to me."

"I see." He nodded. "Except your source got it wrong. It's not a movie. They're coming out to film ranch life and take a few pictures. In and out. No big deal."

"They don't need any extras?"

"Extra? Extra what?"

"You know. Like actors. Walk-on parts." She offered him a knowing smile. "I had high hopes of becoming an actress myself, once upon a time."

Joe ran a hand over his face. "Bitsy, I'm telling you, it's not a movie."

"If you say so, Joe." She glanced down at the lights

on the desk phone. "He's done. Let me buzz him." She picked up the receiver. "Joe Gallagher here to see you, boss."

Moments later, Sam Lawson came out of his office and crossed his arms over his chest. "I thought we agreed you wouldn't call me 'boss' anymore."

Bitsy shrugged. "Coffee's fresh."

The sheriff's expression made no effort to conceal what he thought about the coffee. Joe nearly burst out laughing.

"No, thanks," Sam finally said. He looked to Joe. "Come on in."

The two men walked into his office. Sam shut the door and took a deep breath. "The woman would try a saint. No doubt she's listening at the door right now," he muttered.

"I figured as much."

Sam turned on the tower fan in the corner.

"You're warm?" Joe asked.

"White noise. She can't hear us when the fan is on."

"Ever thought about replacing her?"

"Only about three dozen times a day, for the last four years." His eyes narrowed. "But that's for cowards. I am no coward. My plan is to wait her out. She has to retire eventually." Sam sat down behind his desk and took a deep breath. "What can I do for you?"

"Rebecca Simpson is back in town," Joe said as he eased into the banged-up oak chair.

"The woman who was in all the newspapers? I heard she was found innocent."

Joe's head jerked up. "What are you talking about?"

"Rebecca Simpson. Isn't that who we're discussing? I've never met her, but I read about it in the *Denver Post*."

"Read about what?" Joe asked, becoming as agitated as he was confused.

"The accident."

"What accident?"

"Are you telling me you don't know?" Sam rubbed his chin. "Rebecca Simpson was arrested for vehicular manslaughter. She was driving in the rain when the vehicle skidded, ran off the road and overturned. Her husband Nick wasn't wearing a seat belt. The news said he was killed on impact."

The air whooshed from Joe's lungs and he froze, unable to speak for moments. Finally he cleared his throat. "That doesn't sound like vehicular manslaughter to me."

"Exactly what the jury decided. Her father-in-law, Judge Nicholas Brown, was the one who insisted she be charged."

He shook his head. "How did I miss this?"

"Two-and-a-half years ago, you were in Afghanistan. Then your dad died." He nodded toward Joe's prosthesis. "Your arm. I don't suppose reading the Denver paper was on your radar, although by then they were probably onto something else."

"Hard to believe my mother didn't mention anything."

"Maybe she thought you had enough on your plate."

Joe released a breath. "I guess."

"Did you know Nick Simpson?" Sam asked.

"No. Though it was hard to avoid the gossip when he and Becca eloped. His parents have a summer home near Four Forks. He went to boarding school out East. I hear he spent most of his summers doing whatever it is that rich kids do in the summer. Never saw him in Paradise."

"How'd she meet him?"

"College. Becca had a full ride to Colorado College. I

went local. We ranch boys like to stay close to home, so we can smell the loam in our own backyard."

"Is that how it works? Didn't someone tell me you two used to be an item?"

"We were kids. Too long ago to even remember." Joe shifted in his seat. "So what do you think about the accident?"

"I don't know what to think, Joe. Why wasn't a smart guy like that wearing his seat belt was my first question."

Joe shook his head, thinking.

Sam shrugged. "Truth is, I can't tell you anything that wasn't in the news or on the television. I remember thinking at the time that the whole situation seemed sensationalized to sell more papers."

The only sound for moments was the hum of the fan as Joe considered the information Sam had shared, while trying to piece it all together.

"Funny how one moment can define the course of your entire life," Sam finally said.

"Tell me about it." Joe stood. "Thanks for your time."

"Sure. I can't say I've told you anything everyone else doesn't already know. You can probably read the newspaper account at the library." Sam stood as well and came around his desk.

Joe nodded.

"Any idea if she's here to stay?" Sam asked.

"To stay? No idea. She's doing the certification on my prosthesis. That's all I know."

"Is there a problem?"

"I thought there was. The real-estate agent refused to rent her a house."

"You think Judge Brown could be behind that?"

"I'm not sure."

"Do you want me to investigate?" Sam asked.

"No. But thanks, Sam. After what you told me, I'm sort of looking forward to figuring this one out myself."

Chapter Two

"**M**omma!" Casey Simpson raced across the lawn, her dark braids bouncing as she moved. When she got close, she launched herself into her mother's arms.

Rebecca buried her face in her daughter's neck, breathing in the sweet scent.

"I've missed you so much, Momma."

"I've missed you, too, baby."

"Grandma's in the house. I'll get her."

A moment later, the front screen creaked open, then closed with a bang, causing Rebecca to look up. Joan Anshaw stood on the front porch of the gray clapboard house. "I thought you'd never get here."

"I was starting to feel the same way. That old Honda is on its last legs."

Her mother pushed back a strand of her short dark bob, and took off her glasses to wipe the moisture from her eyes. "Oh, Mom, don't cry." Rebecca moved quickly to the porch, wrapping her mother in a warm embrace.

"I'm not crying."

"You're not?" Rebecca peered down into the face of the woman who had been her rock for the last twenty-four months.

"No. Cowgirls don't cry. Remember? Your daddy always said that."

Ah, her father. Rebecca smiled at the memory. Her dad, Jackson Anshaw, had spent most of his life as foreman for Hollis Elliott Ranch Holdings.

"Daddy only said that so I'd stop whining about all the chores he gave me."

Joan laughed. "It worked, didn't it?" She sniffed before slipping her glasses back on.

"Yes, it did." She pressed a kiss to her mother's cheek. "We're in the homestretch now, Mom. Let's not forget that." She smiled. "I am so grateful for OrthoBorne Technology for giving me my job back and this opportunity. Just the fact that we don't live four hours from each other is a blessing."

"Does that mean you're here in Paradise to stay?"

"One step at a time. I have custody of my daughter again. I have a job, and I'm here until Joe Gallagher finishes certification." Rebecca smiled, savoring the thought of being in the same place as her mother and her daughter for a while.

"What then?" her mother asked.

"Then the company will decide if I can be promoted to full-time senior case manager. With that position, I can work from home. I'd touch base with the Denver offices once a week."

"Oh, Bec, that would be wonderful. Casey wouldn't have to change schools again."

"I know. There's a lot riding on this assignment, not to mention a fat bonus check."

Joan sank onto one of the rocking chairs on the porch. She tucked her slim, denim-clad legs beneath her. "So what's the plan?"

Rebecca leaned back against the porch railing. "I start at Gallagher Ranch on Monday."

"Wonderful."

"Yes. And I'm still looking for a place for the summer."

"I thought you had a rental."

"That fell through."

"Fell through? That's odd. You don't think Nick's grandfather had something to do with it, do you?"

"Let's not go there." Rebecca shook her head. She refused to let Judge Brown put a cloud on all the good things that were happening. "I'll be making a few calls on Monday. Something will open up."

"You know you can stay with me," her mother said. "Casey will be here after school and during the day in the summer anyhow."

"I appreciate all you're doing, but it's really important for me to establish a home for myself and Casey." She pushed her hair back. "You've raised her the last two years while we've been waiting for the case to go to trial."

"I was glad to be able to help."

"And I'm grateful, but I don't want her to forget I'm her mother. Besides, you deserve a little time for yourself. You've given up everything for me, and the least I can do is give you your life back. It's time for you to just enjoy being a grandmother."

"Grandma?"

Rebecca and her mother turned to see Casey standing inside the house, her face pressed against the door screen looking out at them. "May I go next door to see if the twins can come out to play?"

Joan opened her mouth and then paused. She looked to Rebecca. "Honey, you need to ask your mother."

Casey looked back and forth between the two adults, her brows knit. "Momma?"

"Who are the twins?"

"My best friends. We go to school together."

"Well, then, sure. Go ahead," Rebecca said.

"Thank you, Momma." Casey pushed open the door and then raced down the stairs.

Rebecca turned to her mother. "Thank you."

"I suppose it is confusing for her. I hadn't considered that."

"It's all going to work out."

Her mother met her gaze. "Rebecca, do you really think this is finally behind you?"

She stepped forward and knelt next to her mother's chair, reaching out to wrap her hands around her mom's. "I have made a commitment to the Lord to stop looking at how far I have to go. I need focus on how far I've come instead."

Joan nodded slowly. "You're absolutely right."

"I want you to do the same. Promise me, Mom."

"I will, but you know it's hard. Casey is your baby, and you'll always be mine. I hurt when you hurt." She reached up to gently place her hands on either side of her daughter's face. "Even though you were far away in Denver, don't think I haven't read between the lines these past years. I always suspected there was a problem. I should have pushed harder, even when you denied anything was wrong."

Rebecca bit her lip, her eyes shuttering closed for a brief moment, all the while rhythmically rubbing her right arm, as her mother continued. Yes, she could recall the too many times that she visited her mother, all the while disguising the bruises and scars on her arm with long sleeves. Or answering a phone call while holding back tears and pretending everything was perfectly fine when it wasn't.

"All I knew to do was to get down on my knees and pray," Joan continued.

"Oh, Mom." Rebecca's voice cracked, and she paused to swallow hard. "I thank God every single day that I have a mother like you."

Joe glanced at the clock. Nearly nine a.m. He'd finished his Monday morning chores in record time before heading back to the house to shower and wait for Becca.

Reaching in his drawer for a clean white undershirt, his hand touched a box in the back of the bureau. Joe pulled it out. *The ring.* Twelve years ago he'd withdrawn everything out of savings to purchase the silver band with the solitaire diamond. His plan was to propose after college graduation, in the spring, his favorite time of year. He'd be working full-time at the ranch again, and he'd hoped Becca would transfer to a college close by.

Yeah, that was the idea.

Only Becca had married Nick Simpson.

He should have sold the ring right then and there. Bought a car maybe. Except he couldn't do it. Instead he kept it to remind himself that he didn't know a thing about women back then, and he sure hadn't learned anything since.

Shoving the box out of sight, Joe yanked an undershirt and a sweatshirt from the open drawer.

A glance in the mirror confirmed that he wore a permanent frown on his face, but there wasn't a thing he could do at the moment to change that. It wasn't just the weather souring his disposition. He'd hardly slept last night knowing that Becca would be back today. That meant that he'd have to show her his arm.

Why was he nervous? No big deal, right? After all, she worked for the prosthesis company. Seeing amputees and amputations was part of her job on a daily basis. Only this wasn't just another day in Paradise for him. His stomach churned at the thought of being fully exposed, figuratively, as well as literally. No one had seen his arm since the accident, except medical professionals. He'd made sure of that. Yeah, she was a medical professional, except this was different. It was Becca.

Would she be as repulsed as he was at the sight of his misshapen flesh? The residual limb was a shameful, daily reminder of his mistake and all he'd lost.

Joe groaned as he rubbed the taut muscles at the base of his neck. He needed coffee. Lots of coffee and he needed it now. Java might soothe the beast rumbling inside him. He headed to the kitchen where the coffeepot's spitting noises indicated the brew was nearly ready.

The doorbell rang. Without thinking, he reached for the glass carafe with his left hand. He fumbled, causing the hot, dark liquid to slosh over the lip of the container onto the counter. In seconds it became a moving stream that raced to the tile floor.

It took an effort to bite back angry words. Shoving the carafe back into place, Joe tossed a towel onto the dark puddle on the floor and headed out of the room, nearly tripping over his brother's black lab, Millie, on the way.

He swung open the front door. As his gaze met Becca's through the screen, the building irritation that stalked him diffused. She wore a crisp blue shirt with *OrthoBorne* stitched on the pocket, and dark slacks, with a rolling briefcase at her side. Her long hair had been pulled back into a ponytail. Dressed like a professional, and she was bright-eyed and chipper to boot.

"Hey, Becca."

"Joe."

"Find the place all right?" He folded his arms across his chest. The residual limb remained hidden in the folds of his long-sleeve shirt, just the way he liked.

Becca cleared her throat and nodded. "Yes. I did. Thank you."

Joe held open the door and nodded an invitation into the house. He was grateful the cleaning lady had been by on Friday. Everything still sparkled. High oak-beamed ceilings and polished oak floors made the interior appear huge. The décor had a Southwest theme, but the place was minimalist, like him.

"Beautiful room."

"Thanks," he muttered.

She turned her head and smiled. "Who do we have here?"

Joe followed her gaze. Dan's dog padded into the room. The animal looked at them with baleful eyes.

"This is Millie."

Millie whined, nudging Becca's leg until she reached down to rub her ears. "Oh, goodness, isn't she sweet?"

"She's neurotic."

"Excuse me?"

"Separation anxiety. She's been like this since Dan and my mother left. The dog is driving me crazy."

Becca tilted her head, and her ponytail swayed with the movement as she assessed Joe. "You do seem a little out of sorts. Do you want to reschedule?"

"No. Let's get this over with." He nodded toward the kitchen. "This way."

Becca grabbed her briefcase handle and followed him down a short hall to a spacious kitchen, the wheels clicking on the tile floor.

"Coffee?" he asked.

"No, thank you." She stopped, her gaze drawn to the mess on the floor. "What happened?"

"I got into a little argument with the coffeemaker."

"I hate when that happens."

Before he realized it, she had reached for a roll of paper towels on the counter. Joe insinuated himself between her and the spilled coffee.

"I don't need help."

"Sorry," she murmured.

Joe carefully mopped up the counter, then the floor before pouring coffee into his travel mug and sealing the lid. "Would it be okay to work at the kitchen table? I have the prosthesis charging there."

"Sure." Becca glanced at the table and then the room.

Joe glanced around, as well. He was proud of the place. The same oak beams overhead dominated the room and held an oak ceiling fan with rows of recessed lights. The kitchen itself was oak, with stainless steel appliances and black granite countertops. The room lacked clutter, and that was exactly the way he liked things.

"You built this place?"

Joe shrugged. "Can't say I built anything. My job was to nod a lot. Somehow I ended up with this." He walked to the table and set down his mug. When he lifted his gaze, Becca was intently watching him. "What?"

"Nothing. I didn't expect…"

"Didn't expect a poor cowboy to have a place like this?"

"That's not what I meant, Joe." She took a deep breath, then opened her briefcase and placed a thick file on the table along with her tablet computer. "Do you mind if I take a look at your residual limb?"

"Have at it." Joe pulled off his sweatshirt and offered

her his right upper extremity. He held his breath for moments, but she didn't flinch or grimace as he'd expected.

Becca's hands were soft and cool upon his skin as she examined first the biceps, then the triceps of the limb before moving to the slightly puckered, scarred incision line and the skin on either side of the amputation. She dappled her fingers along the entire surface, her gaze intent. Finally she looked up.

"Sensitivity?"

Joe shook his head in denial because he'd been just fine a minute ago. Until she touched him.

When she began to type notes in her tablet, Joe was unable to look away. He found himself assessing her concentrated effort as she worked. The ponytail shifted, exposing her neck and the curve of her face.

Becca raised her eyes, and her pupils widened as she caught him staring. With a flip of her fingers, she moved a wayward lock of hair behind her ear, then cleared her throat.

"Pain or phantom pain?"

"Nothing a couple ibuprofen won't fix."

"You've been doing your exercises and taking very good care of the area. The muscles are in excellent shape, and the skin tone and the incision line are very healthy. All in all, it looks beautiful."

"Beautiful?" The tension in him eased. "Is that a medical term?"

"Would you prefer, 'incision line healed, edges well approximated, clean and free of exudate, swelling or edema'?"

"Beautiful it is."

"Obviously you followed your surgeon's instructions to a T."

"I'm pretty good at following orders. The army will do that to you."

"The army? Right. I forgot about the army. Though, your upper body strength is indicative of more than following instructions."

"I have a small gym set up in one of the bedrooms. I can't afford any further setbacks."

"Any other learning-curve issues with the left hand?"

"Yeah. A few. Roping cows. Brushing my teeth. Shaving with a razor remains an interesting experience. I had a beard for a long time, just to keep me from bleeding all over the place."

"Too bad I didn't come out here sooner. I could have saved you a couple pints of blood." She smiled. "Anything else?"

"Still have the occasional clumsy episode, as you can see." He nodded toward the spilled coffee.

"We all have the occasional clumsy episode in the morning, Joe." She picked up the two pieces of his prosthesis he had ready on the table and inspected them. "Do you want to go ahead and don this?"

He massaged antiseptic lubricant into the area and examined the cosmetic silicone glove for damage. Then he disconnected the charger from his myoelectric prosthesis, snapped together the hand and forearm and applied the device to what remained of his right arm.

He held it up for her review. "There you go. Bionic man reporting for duty."

"Are you always this hard on yourself?" she murmured.

"I deserve to be hard on myself. I messed up. I should have asked for help, as everyone keeps reminding me. If I had, I wouldn't have this. I'd be normal. A normal rancher."

Her jaw sagged slightly as she stared at him. "I don't know what to say to that."

"What's there to say? I'm not the guy I used to be."

"That's not true, and believe me, normal is highly overrated."

"Becca, I'm sure most people appreciate platitudes, but I deal in reality and I'm sorry, but you don't know what you're talking about."

She stiffened. "Joe, your arm doesn't define you."

"Sure it does."

"You're wrong. You're a person who happens to be an amputee. That integral person inside is what people imprint in their minds when they define who you are." She stared past him. "No matter how hard something else tries to change a person's core, it generally doesn't change."

"What exactly is my core, Becca?"

When she met his gaze, she reached out to lay a hand on his arm.

Joe moved from her touch.

The rebuff only seemed to make her more determined to make her point, and she leaned closer.

"You're an intelligent, kind, godly man."

"Are you sure you're not confusing me with someone else? God and I haven't been buddies for some time, and I'm not as kind as you like to think." He shook his head. "Sometimes our mind blocks out the not-so-memorable things about people we haven't seen in a long time. We tend to remember people in a skewed positive light. I'm not that boy from high school."

"Trust me. I don't have that problem. I'm cynical enough to remember everything from the past." Becca chuckled softly. "I'm absolutely certain you haven't changed as much as you'd like to believe." She refused to give him eye contact; instead, she reached for her tablet, her fingers sliding across the keys on the screen once again.

"It's been over a year since your accident. You began prosthesis fittings and training six months ago. Why didn't you complete certification then?"

"It's taken me a while to actually commit to the whole prosthesis thing. After the accident and a couple of surgeries and rehab and all, I'd already been going back and forth to Denver so many times for preprosthetic therapy, and interim prosthetic therapy, that my head was spinning. I admit I didn't adhere to the usual patient guidelines."

"You aren't exactly the usual patient," she said.

"Bingo." He took a deep breath. "Dan ran the ranch and my mother helped. I needed to take that load from them as soon as possible."

"Is your mother still living in the main house?"

"Yeah. She and my niece just left for California. They've gone to visit my sisters, then meet up with Dan and his wife."

"Dan's married?"

"Yeah. Sort of a newlywed, too. He postponed his honeymoon for me."

"That's a great brother." She paused, thinking. "Family is everything, isn't it?"

"Yeah. Sometimes it's the only thing that gets me through the day."

"And faith," she said softly, her eyes averted.

"Truthfully, I'm not sure what faith is anymore." Joe cleared his throat. "No disrespect. I know you've been through a lot, and if your faith is what helped you, then good for you."

"Good for me?" She offered a scoffing laugh. When

she met his gaze, her eyes were hard and unflinching. "But we're not here to talk about me, are we?"

He nodded. "Understood."

"I need you to fill out this paperwork."

Joe groaned. "More paperwork? OrthoBorne is big on it, aren't they?" He glanced at the clock. "Could we save that for another session? I'm getting behind on my day."

"I promise this is the last of it."

He looked her in the eye. "You know what's been the most difficult part of this transition?"

"What's that?"

"Learning to write with my left hand. I'll do anything to get out of paper shuffling."

Becca paused. "We are in the field. I'm willing to compromise. We can skip that and go straight to shadowing. However, don't be surprised if I come up with some unique teaching sessions while I'm shadowing you."

"Deal." He looked at her. "What do you mean by shadowing?"

"That means that I show up tomorrow and follow you around for a couple of days, asking you the questions. I basically need to document the tasks that make up the majority of your workday so I can create a plan of care for your specific occupational therapy."

"I get up at four thirty, and I'm ready to start the day at five.

"Seriously?"

"Too early for you?"

"No. I meant you're okay with me following you around from dawn to dusk for a few days?"

"I'll do anything to avoid wasting my time—" he glanced with distaste at the paperwork "—checking little boxes and writing answers to inane questions. But five seems a little early for someone who isn't punching a clock."

"I understand my job, thank you. This is all about getting to know your world. So if you start your day at five, so do I, at least to start with."

"Fair enough. I'll meet you at the barn." He glanced at her outfit. "You do have boots, right?"

"Yes. Several pairs, in fact."

"Ranch boots. We're not talking city girl, fancy boots."

"Yes, ranch boots. You seem to forget that I worked on a ranch with my father practically my whole life."

"I didn't forget." He paused. "But people change."

"I'm still the same ranch girl I was twelve years ago."

"I guess we'll see," Joe murmured.

"I guess we will," Becca answered without missing a beat. She closed the cover on her tablet.

"What time does your crew arrive?"

"Nine thirty."

"They're late," he observed with a glance at the big stainless-steel clock on the wall.

"I don't want to keep you from your chores." She began to pack up her briefcase. "I'll wait outside for them."

"You're welcome to wait in the house."

"Oh, no. I'll wait outside."

"Your call." He reached for his keys, with his left hand, and fumbled. The keys clattered to the oak floor.

An awkward silence ensued as they both stared at the ground between them.

"I got 'em." Joe scooped up the keys with his other hand and shoved them in his pocket.

"Do you mind if I give you a little impromptu lesson?" Becca asked.

"Okay," he said slowly.

"You're using the myoelectric hand statically."

"Pardon me?"

"Static. Like a placeholder. I've observed your hand mostly in the relaxed position. You have quite a few positions available. Utilize them. The more you do, the more it will be automatic. Like the lateral pinch. You could have picked up the keys that way." She demonstrated, putting her own keys on the table. "See how much more accurate?"

He nodded. "I'll, ah, give it a try."

"I hope you will. Why not maximize the technology? After all, it's yours, and the photographer will want to see you taking advantage of their product."

Becca was right. He might not be paying for the prosthesis in cash, but he was paying for it by agreeing to OrthoBorne's offer. And he had been pretty much ignoring the technology, thinking maybe if he did, maybe he could ignore the fact that he was an amputee.

All he'd really wanted was for life to go back to the way it was before the accident. It suddenly occurred to him that maybe his way wasn't working. Maybe the Lord had other plans despite the fact that he'd been ignoring Him, as well.

But was he ready for what was in store?

Chapter Three

Rebecca leaned against her Honda. She checked her watch and then focused her gaze on the main road. Late was an understatement. Joe had been gone two hours. Her stomach growled, and she wondered what the day's special was at Patti Jo's Café and Bakery in downtown Paradise.

Things with Joe had gone better than she expected. He wasn't nearly as surly this morning as he'd been on Saturday at their unexpected reunion. She pushed away the worrisome thoughts that hovered nearby. This was going to work out. It had to.

That was, if the team would show up. She pulled her cell from her pocket to call the OrthoBorne offices in Denver. When she looked up, a big white pickup truck, with rooftop bar lights and the logo of the Paradise Sheriff's Department, appeared on the road to the ranch, moving to the arched entrance. Behind it was a black SUV, kicking up a cloud of dust on the gravel road.

A police escort to the ranch?

She hurried to the drive and met the sheriff's vehicle as it pulled up.

The uniformed officer unfolded his tall form and

stepped out and placed a tan Stetson on his head. "I'm Sam Lawson." He reached out to grasp her hand in a strong handshake. "You must be Rebecca Simpson." His eyes were warm with welcome.

"Yes. How did you know?"

"Joe mentioned you." He nodded toward the car pulling in behind his truck. "These folks say they're from OrthoBorne Technology in Denver. Sound right to you?"

"Yes. They're Joe's media team."

"I found them driving through town. After the third pass through, I decided to take pity on them. According to the driver, they were here an hour ago, at another gate, but couldn't find the road."

"Thanks for bringing them here, Sheriff."

"Better not thank me. This crew is greener than the grass, and I'm feeling guilty for delivering them to the ranch. In fact, maybe you could not mention to Joe that I brought them."

She laughed.

"Oh, sure, you're laughing now, but you won't be when you figure out that I'm right." He waved as he left.

A tall man in his midforties got out of the SUV. He shook his head and released a breath. "Gallagher Ranch, I hope."

"It is, and I'm Rebecca Simpson."

"Our liaison, right?"

"Yes. I'm also doing the certification."

"Great. I'm Rod, photographer and videographer." He stepped forward to offer a grin of relief, along with a brisk handshake.

She took his hand while returning the smile.

"Looks like we're all in the family. OrthoBorne family, that is. Sorry we're so late. The GPS on the rental went wacky once we hit the outskirts of town. We thought we were here once, but there was no road beyond the gate. For all I know, we were on another ranch somewhere around here."

"No worries," Rebecca said. "The good news is after the first time, you won't forget your way to the ranch. It's pretty easy. There's only one paved road in and out of Paradise. Take it until you come to the arched entrance." She pointed to the wrought-iron archway with the large entwined letters *G* and *R*.

"Easy. Yeah, that's what I said until the third or fourth time we passed Patti Jo's Café and Bakery, and I realized I was driving in circles." He turned to the vehicle, giving a wave for the other occupants to join him. "I brought Julian, our intern, and Abigail, one of our staff copywriters."

"Mr. Gallagher didn't mention three of you."

"Julian was a last-minute addition," Rod said. "He'll assist with shoots."

The front passenger door of the vehicle swung open, and a tall, thin, young man with long shaggy hair, a minuscule beard and wire-rim glasses rolled out. Earphones were propped on his head. When he glanced around, enthusiasm brightened his eyes. "Wow. This is great. I've never been west of the mountains."

The only female of the group came around the truck to assess the situation. With one hand, she shoved back her shoulder-length cascade of strawberry-blond hair and with the other she pushed an oversized black leather tote over her shoulder.

"I knew we were in Paradise the minute I laid eyes on the good sheriff." The woman smiled and stepped forward, offering a handshake in greeting. Her nails were short and unpolished, no-nonsense like the woman herself, who was dressed in tan khakis and a taupe sweater. "Abigail Warren. Call me Abi."

"Rebecca Simpson."

"Yes," Abi said quietly. "I've read about you."

"Don't believe everything you read," Rebecca murmured in response.

"Never. I'm a writer. I recognize fiction when I see it."

When Abi winked, Rebecca knew she'd found an ally.

Overhead the sky rumbled. "Uh-oh." Julian tugged the earphones from his head to listen closely. "Thunder? That can't be good."

"Let's move over to the horse barn. It's the closest shelter." Rebecca pointed to the large red building. "The log cabin to your left is Mr. Gallagher's, and that two-story colonial on your right is the main house."

When the sky thundered again, the crew picked up their pace, following Rebecca. Along the way, their curious gazes took in the details of the Gallagher ranch, the barn, the fenced-in corral and the utility garage.

"Is that a windmill?" Abi asked, pointing to the teetering, metal structure standing out in the distance.

"It is."

"What do they use them for?" she asked.

"They used to be utilized to bring water from the aquifers to the cattle. Most ranches use pump irrigation now."

"When will we meet our client?" Rod asked.

"That depends on when he comes back from the pasture."

"Horses," Julian said when Rebecca pulled open one of the large barn doors. Wonderment laced his voice. He turned around to observe the stalls.

"That's probably why she called it a horse barn," Abi noted.

"This is Julian's first big on-location assignment," Rod

said. "His life is usually spent working with computer software in the office. Generally his idea of nature is the Denver Zoo."

Julian shrugged. "I'd deny it, except it's absolutely true."

"Great, then you'll appreciate that we're going to tour the ranch first thing tomorrow."

"It's starting to rain." Julian observed the fat drops beginning to touch the ground.

"Rain doesn't stop life on the ranch," Rebecca said.

She scrutinized their clothing, from Abi's open toe sandals to Julian's flip-flops and realized that it was actually a very good thing that Joe wasn't here.

"Let's talk about your schedule, and then I'll let you get back to town to check in at the Paradise Bed and Breakfast and do some shopping."

"Shopping?" Abi perked up.

"Yes." Rebecca smiled. "First, I'd like to take this opportunity to make a few safety recommendations." She stared pointedly at Julian. "Leave your earphones and earbuds in your suitcase. While you are working on the ranch, it's important to listen and be in tune with your surroundings. You'll want to hear the nuances of the land, including the weather. There are potential dangers, as well."

"Dangers?" Julian asked.

"Dangerous wildlife, or even a ranch animal in distress."

Rod nodded as the others focused on her words.

"You need boots. Cowboy boots, hiking boots or sturdy rubber boots with safety toes. Whatever you prefer. They'll protect your feet and ankles from things like horse hooves, cow patties, insects, or even snakebites.

Besides boots, you'll want to dress in layers. It's cold in the morning, warm in the afternoon."

"I'd really like a cowboy hat," Abi said.

Rebecca chuckled. "You do need some sort of hat. A cowboy hat is perfect. Gloves, sunscreen. All a necessity. Our altitude is higher than Denver's. You can get burned faster here than in the city."

"Anything else?" Rod asked.

"Tomorrow we'll start by driving around the ranch, so bring your gear and water bottles. Keep in mind that there are no restrooms out in the pasture."

"Any place to charge a cell phone?" Julian asked as he held his phone aloft in various positions, searching for reception.

Rebecca blinked. "I imagine we'll be using a ranch truck, or utility vehicle, and usually ranch vehicles are of the ancient variety. It probably doesn't have an adapter." She paused. "I can't even guarantee one bar out here. Most days in the warm months, yes. But you never know. It all depends on Mother Nature and where you happen to be standing."

"You're on the wild prairie," Rod said with a chuckle.

"Your priority needs to be hydration. We're at nearly nine thousand feet above sea level, which beats the 5,280 of the Mile-High City. If you aren't sufficiently hydrated, you'll get headaches, feel faint and possibly pass out. You're Coloradans. You know the drill."

Julian took another swig from his water bottle.

"Try not to get between Mr. Gallagher and his chores. I can't emphasize that enough. This is a working ranch. One that he manages pretty much solo."

"We're going to want to follow Gallagher around for at least a full day," Rod said. "Then we can go back later to set up some specific shoots."

"I figured you'd want to shadow him."

"What time should we be out here?" Rod asked.

"Five a.m. is the time he gave me. Sunrise is at five thirty."

"In the morning?" Julian squeaked.

"The last time I was up at five in the morning I was pulling all-nighters in college," Abi murmured.

"Yeah, but think of the sunrise shots we can get. I imagine the sky is endless out here that time of day."

"Yes. You're right, Rod. Though tomorrow you get a break. I'll be shadowing Mr. Gallagher until eight a.m. I'll meet you in front of the barn at eight thirty, and we can do our tour of the ranch. Keep in mind that it's another twenty minutes from town to the ranch. You'll actually have to be up earlier to get here in time."

"I'm exhausted just thinking about our schedule," Julian said.

Rebecca chuckled. "Welcome to Paradise, folks."

Thunder cracked, and they all jumped, turning in time to see the darkened sky light up with a brilliant flash.

"This cannot be a good sign," Julian murmured.

"They have rain slickers at the tack shop in town," Rebecca offered.

Abi's eyes rounded and she looked past Rebecca, mesmerized. "Who's that?"

Rebecca turned around. From the west, a lone figure rode toward them. A black Stetson on his head, he sat tall and formidable in the saddle.

"That would be Joe Gallagher?" Abi asked.

"My model?" Rod asked with a wide grin on his face.

"It is," Rebecca said.

"And here I thought I was going to be photographing a grizzled old rancher."

"Well done, OrthoBorne," Abi said.

Two dogs appeared, not far behind, racing toward the corrals. As Joe got closer, he raised his left hand to tip the Stetson to the back of his head and narrowed his eyes to assess the strangers on his ranch.

"Uh-oh. Your model doesn't look happy," Abi murmured.

Joe reined in the horse a short distance away and dismounted easily from the saddle. Steely-eyed, he crossed his arms on his broad chest and faced them.

"We have a problem," he said to Rebecca. The words were a slow accusation delivered with a tone that brooked no argument.

"A problem?" She swallowed.

"The paddock and north gate were left open."

"Oops," Julian murmured.

Rod and Abi turned to glare at Julian.

"So it *was* your ranch," Abi said.

"We took a few cow pictures when we were lost," Rod said.

"Bull."

Rod jerked back, his eyes rounding. "Excuse me?"

"That's a bull, not a cow," Joe returned.

"Yes, sir," Rod said with a nod.

Joe narrowed his gaze and looked slowly from Julian, to Rod and then Abi. "You know the first rule of the ranch?"

"Do no harm?" Julian asked.

"That's doctors," Rod said drily.

"Leave everything the way you find it." Joe moved into the barn with his horse.

"Seriously?" Julian said. "I would have never guessed that in a million years."

"Pay attention, Julian. I suspect Mr. Gallagher is trying to tell us something," Rod muttered.

Rebecca raised a hand, indicating for the crew to stay put as she followed Joe into the barn. "Your bull is loose?"

"*Was*. Rowdy crossed the road and knocked down my neighbor's garden fence and trampled his wife's tomato plants. It would have been worse except he's old, and all that exercise wore him out."

"What are you going to do?"

"Already done. Gil and Wishbone helped me herd him back, which put me an hour behind on my chores, not including the fence I still need to repair." He ran a hand over his face. "I'll need to go into town for tomato plants. Oh, and I'll need to add those fancy frost guards to my list. Good old Rowdy smashed those, as well." He let out a weary breath.

"Joe, I'm sorry. I'll have the crew go into town for the plants if that will help."

"This is my ranch. I'll handle it." He met her gaze. "I can tell you what will help. Getting them in and out fast. The longer they're on Gallagher Ranch, the greater the chances are I'm going to lose my temper."

"Yes. Yes. Of course. I'll monitor them more closely and we'll get this done quickly."

"The clock starts ticking now, Becca."

Rebecca offered a solemn nod. He was absolutely right, and she was completely certain that she was going to need some serious prayer time in order to pull off this assignment.

"I'll be back in the morning."

"What?" At the sound of Becca's voice, Joe turned from brushing his horse and stared at her. She stood in the doorway of the barn, hesitation on her face.

"To shadow you." She rubbed her right arm for a moment, then stopped, as if realizing what she was doing, and slipped her hands into the pockets of her jeans.

Joe put the curry comb on the shelf. He glanced at his watch, a decision already made in his mind. "Come on, then. I only have a few minutes."

"A few minutes?"

"Lunch and a trip into town are next on my list."

Becca followed him as he left the barn. Overhead the sky continued to spit, and dark clouds rumbled. He moved to the gravel drive.

"I don't follow. A few minutes for what?"

"The truck." Joe nodded toward the used-to-be-black, muddy farm truck. He unlocked and opened the passenger door for her before getting in on his side.

"Yes. But where are we going?"

He didn't answer but continued down a well-worn dirt road to the south, right behind the barn. Less than two minutes later, he pulled up in front of a small cottage with a simple rail porch. Large weathered terra-cotta pots had been placed along the brick walkway that led to the porch steps. They were ready for planting.

"What's this?" Becca asked.

Joe played with the leather cover on the steering wheel, avoiding her eyes. "It'll be easier to monitor what's going on if you stay at the ranch."

"What?" She looked from the house and back to him. He gave a nod of affirmation.

"Oh, no, I could never impose." The words came quickly as she shook her head.

He focused straight ahead at the mud-spattered windshield, now blurred with drops of rain. "You wouldn't be imposing. No one is using this place. It's been empty since last September."

"Whose house is it?"

"Dan lived here with his daughter before he got married. The place is furnished, too."

"But—"

"This is strictly a business agreement. I need to complete certification, and having you close by will ensure that will happen as quickly as you've promised. Especially since you have to babysit greenhorns, who seem to have a knack for stepping in cow patties everywhere they go."

She paused, considering his words. "What about Casey?"

"Who's Casey?"

"My daughter."

Joe's jaw sagged. "You have a daughter?"

"I do. She's six."

"Yeah. Of course your daughter is welcome."

Becca stared at him for moments, confusion on her face. Then her eyes widened. "Is this about the rental deal falling through?" She released a small gasp. "You overheard the entire conversation, didn't you?"

"I heard enough. Doesn't change the facts."

She turned away. "Of course it does."

"Why? I told you, this is business."

When she didn't say anything, he muttered a short expression under his breath. *Stubborn.* He'd forgotten how stubborn the woman could be when her back was against the wall.

"Becca, don't let your pride stand in the way."

"It's not my pride. I'm used to that being shredded." She met his gaze for a moment, then shifted her attention out the window. "I...don't think you understand what's going on here, Joe."

"Going on? What do you mean?"

"Letting me stay on your ranch may put you right in the center of the bull's-eye." She gestured with her hands.

"You aren't making any sense."

"Why do you think I didn't get that rental house?" Rebecca asked.

"I have a few ideas."

"So do I. Nick's grandfather. I'm sure of it. Judge Nicholas Brown used his considerable influence to sway the courts to bring what was simply a horrible car accident to a jury trial."

Joe opened his mouth and closed it again, his lips forming a thin line.

"My bail was set so high that my mother was left scrambling to raise the money. I sat in jail for two weeks. *Two weeks.* Do you know what it's like to be in jail, Joe?" She swallowed. "Do you have any idea?"

Hands tightening on the steering wheel, Joe's head jerked back as though he'd been hit.

She took a steadying breath. "When Hollis Elliott heard about it, he put up the bond money."

"I don't get it. You were found innocent."

"Judge Brown continues to punish mc for Nick's death."

"Why, if it was an accident?"

"Not in his mind." She twisted her hands in her lap. "I think he's aiming for custody of my daughter."

"He has no grounds for that."

"Rich people live in a different world than you and me. He's a prominent citizen in the valley. He owns a lot of property in Four Forks. He'll claim he can better provide for Casey." She released a breath. "The truth is that he can."

"You're her mother. You're employed, and now you have a place to call home."

Rebecca shook her head as she gazed with longing at the little house. "You don't know the judge," she murmured. Her hands trembled as she met his gaze yet again. "If I stay here, he might very well retaliate against you. Against Gallagher Ranch, as well. You need to know that up front."

"I'm not concerned about Judge Brown."

"You also need to know that I'm not looking for someone to rescue me. The Lord and I have been working together for some time now."

He shook his head. "Not applying for the job. This offer is all about me. I've given a crew of city slickers carte blanche to roam my ranch. All I'm trying to do is protect my interests. I can't do that without your help. Living closer makes sense."

"Just so we know where we stand."

He held out the keys to the little cottage with his left hand. "I know where I stand. Do you?"

She nodded, then slowly, ever so slowly, reached up and took the keys, her fingers brushing his.

Joe let out the breath he didn't realize he'd been holding.

Chapter Four

Rebecca turned when she heard the front door of Joe's two-story log-cabin house open behind her.

It was the man himself. Joe placed his black Stetson on his head and slid his arms into the sleeves of a fleece-lined denim jacket as he stepped outside.

The dark angles of his face were illuminated by the porch light, creating a fierce image of the indomitable rancher. He yawned and rubbed a hand over the stubble on his face before raising his head. Joe's eyes rounded when he saw her. "What are you doing out here?"

She ignored the harsh note of surprise in his voice. "I'm here to do a job."

"Why didn't you knock on the door? How long have you been waiting?"

Rebecca shrugged. "There was no need to bother you. I've only been here a few minutes."

"When are you moving into the cottage?"

"Friday. After Casey's school lets out for the summer break."

"What will your daughter do while you're working?" Joe asked.

"My mother will keep her during the week and I will

have Casey here on the weekends. That will be less disruptive while the crew is filming or photographing you."

"You're sure that's going to work?"

"Yes. This is far better than when I lived in Denver and she lived here with my mother all of the time."

He shook his head and frowned as though he waged a mental battle.

"Everything okay?" she asked.

"Yeah. Perfect." He strode to the end of the cobblestone walk and paused to take a deep breath. "Smell that?" he asked.

"What?"

"That heavy, dank odor in the air. The smell of cow manure and pond water are magnified when a low pressure system moves in." He took another deep breath. "Oh, yeah, that's some strong manure on the wind. It won't be just dry lightning like last night, either. No, we have a real storm front on its way."

"I guess I've been gone too long. Nothing smells different to me."

"Give it a few more weeks. We'll have your smeller sensitized in no time."

"Sensitize my smeller?" Rebecca smiled at the terminology.

She pulled a pair of worn, soft leather gloves from her back pocket. When she looked up, he was watching her.

"Those look like expensive gloves. Do you want a pair of old ranch gloves?"

"I'm good."

"And you're going to be warm enough in that vest?"

Rebecca assessed her black, down-filled vest. "You bet. I've got several layers on beneath this."

"Hat?"

"I've got a ball cap in my pocket," she said.

"You need a proper Western hat to protect you from the elements."

"This isn't my first rodeo. I'll be fine."

"Your call," Joe replied.

He turned away and she followed, stretching her stride to keep up with his long legs as he headed past the circular gravel drive, across the yard toward the horse barn.

The morning was silent. The only sound was the sizzle of a halogen light overhead as it came to life, casting a pink glow on the yard. Rebecca glanced up and stared at the endless black carpet of night sky, illuminated only by the scattering blanket of glittering stars.

"Everything okay?" Joe called out.

"Yes, yes. Sorry." Rebecca doubled her pace in his direction. "I forgot what it was like."

He shot her a questioning glance. "New moon, you mean?"

"That, too. But I'd forgotten how amazing a ranch is before dawn."

"I don't even notice anymore. This is all I've ever known. It's a real life, that's for sure. You make me realize how much I take it for granted."

Memories of following her father around Elliott Ranch swirled through Rebecca's mind. She missed her father with a deep ache, but she never thought she'd miss ranch life once she left.

Then again, she'd been wrong about so many things. *Like Nick.* Why should she be surprised?

Joe slid open the barn door and whistled. Two dogs raced to his side. "Meet Gil and Wishbone."

She laughed, offering a bow at the waist. "Gentlemen. Pleased to meet you."

From a corner of the barn a squawking radio sound cut through the silence. Startled, Rebecca jumped. She looked around. "Dispatch radio. I'd forgotten about them."

"Technology moves on, but some things don't change in Paradise. It's still the best backup communication in the agricultural community. Cell phones can't be relied on, and phone lines are iffy with a heavy snow or rainfall."

He strode to a row of stalls.

"Normally I take the truck around the ranch in the morning. That won't be nearly as much fun for you, I imagine."

"I don't want you to deter from your regular schedule."

"The horses could use a good workout, and you'd be doing me a favor. How about if you ride my sister-in-law's horse? She's spirited but not headstrong."

"Your sister-in-law?"

He coughed, biting back a laugh. "The horse."

"Ah." Rebecca offered a short nod while maintaining a poker face. "Whatever you think. You're the boss."

"Need any help with your tack?"

"I'm pretty sure I can handle tacking up my horse. I started doing it when I was five."

"How long since you've ridden?"

"Twelve years," she murmured.

"You'll be sore tomorrow." Joe shook his head. "Tack room is over here."

She glanced around as they entered the small area. Saddles, felt pads and ropes hung neatly on the walls. "This is very nice." She inhaled deeply, attempting to identify the smells. "Leather, castile soap and neatsfoot oil," she said aloud.

"You forgot sweat."

"Yes. That, as well."

Joe handed her a comb and brush and led her to a

far stall, where he opened the door and gently nudged a chestnut mare out into the main area of the barn. "This is Princess."

The horse snorted at the interruption.

"Oh, isn't she a beauty?"

"Sure is, and Beth will appreciate you exercising her mare."

Joe opened another stall and offered the horse inside his palm to sniff, before gently running his hand along the animal's flank and then rubbing him between the ears. "This is Blackie."

"Hi, Blackie."

They worked quietly, cleaning their horses for minutes. When Rebecca looked up, Joe was leaning over the stall rail observing her.

"Why are you smiling?" he asked.

She looked up from where she was bent over Princess's front hoof. "A simple thing like picking hooves. I haven't done it in years, and yet it feels right." Rebecca shook her head. "How did I leave this behind?"

"You tell me." The words were as hard as his expression.

"I don't know," she murmured. Yet she did know. She had stopped listening to her heart and the whispered words from the Lord when she met Nick Simpson. His money and charm had turned her head. He'd offered her a life she thought she'd always wanted. Shame and regret filled Rebecca, and she concentrated on the task once again before finally dusting off her hands.

"All done?" Joe asked minutes later.

"I am, and if you don't mind, since we have the opportunity, I'd like to see how you get that saddle in position with your prosthesis."

"No big deal, now that I've worked on my upper body

strength. Though in truth, it was difficult when I first got home without any prosthesis. I sure wasn't going to wait around for the incision to heal before I rode again."

Of course not. She held back the words. Joe Gallagher hadn't changed that much. He was still stubborn and determined to do things his way.

"Actually I wasn't sure if I would ever ride without assistance, until Dan came up with the idea for a ramp. It has wheels that lock into place with the toes of my boots. It did the job until both my horse and I adjusted to my new situation. Now—" he raised a shoulder in gesture "—I don't need it. It's pretty much business as usual."

He grabbed a saddle pad and carefully placed it on the horse before adding the saddle, positioning them both and tightening the cinch and turning to Becca again.

"Piece of cake," he said.

She followed suit and dropped Princess's stirrups into position. "Now let's see you get yourself in the saddle."

"It's not pretty, but it works."

Joe firmly adjusted the Stetson on his head before he moved to stand on the left side of Blackie. He snugged up on the reins and grabbed the mane with his left hand. Once his left foot was in the stirrup, using his prosthesis, he reached for the saddle horn and then smoothly swung his leg over the horse. The movement was fluid and fast.

"Seriously? You get on your horse slicker than someone with two hands. Best utilization of your prosthesis I've seen yet."

He offered a nod of acknowledgment at the compliment.

"Now what?" Rebecca grabbed Princess's reins and walked the mare outside, right behind him.

Around them the sun had kissed the landscape in a rosy light, illuminating the ranch.

"Look at that." She knew her voice was laced with the awe of a girl who'd lived too long in the city. "'Red sky at morning. Sailors take warning.' Right?"

"That's right," Joe said. "That's not an old wives' tale, either. Red sky at morning is indicative of low stratus clouds, and dust close to the Earth's atmosphere. Another sign a storm is coming."

"I meant that it was beautiful."

He shrugged. "Yeah, that, too."

Rebecca looked out at the land, her gaze moving straight west. "What's the plan? I have two and a half hours before the crew arrives."

"That reminds me." Joe pulled a key from his pocket. He inched his horse close to hers. "Spare key to the farm truck. So you can show them around."

"Thanks."

"I trust you'll read them the ten commandments of ranch life while you're at it?"

"If you mean no repeats of yesterday? Then yes. Absolutely. Along with a couple of rounds of sage cowboy wisdom."

"Cowboy wisdom?" Joe asked.

"Oh, you know. The usual. Look before you step. Don't stand behind a coughing cow."

"That wasn't quite what I meant, but they probably need to hear that, as well."

"Where will you be? I mean in case we need you."

"I've got at least a couple hours of spring pasture maintenance ahead of me before I move the cattle."

"Clearing out the rocks and sticks." She made a face.

"Exactly. Then I'm going into town yet again. I reviewed my contract for this publicity thing last night. They expect me to get a haircut. I don't know how I missed that detail. I could have done it yesterday." He removed his hat and ran a hand over shaggy black hair that skimmed his collar. "Ridiculous. Nothing wrong with my hair."

A smile escaped, as she recalled the time in high school when he'd trusted her to give him a trim. She'd been so tongue-tied and red-faced once she'd run her fingers through his thick hair that she'd given up on the task.

Joe glanced at her and his eyes widened. Was he remembering, as well?

"We better get going," he said gruffly. "We're going to ride the entire fence line before your people show up." He picked up his reins and clicked his tongue. Blackie began to trot forward through the yard.

When he released a long, low whistle for the dogs, Gil and Wishbone came running. "Now I'll get to see if you can still ride," he said, as he adjusted his Stetson. "I'll meet you at the fence."

"Which fence?" Rebecca called after him as she mounted Princess and looked around. "Gallagher Ranch is surrounded by fences."

"We'll start at the one that separates Gallagher Ranch from Elliott Ranch, to the southeast. I know you're familiar with that border. It's the easiest to check because Hollis Elliott has the money to keep up his fences."

"Slow down," she called out. "You started before me."

He turned in the saddle and narrowed his eyes. "Are you telling me you want the handicapped guy to give you a handicap? Doesn't sound like an experienced cowgirl to me."

She blinked, outrage simmering just below the surface. "Careful what you say, Mr. Gallagher. You may have to eat those words."

"I've eaten worse. And this meal is guaranteed to be

tasty." Joe Gallagher's deep laughter filled the morning air.

Rebecca froze at the sound. His spontaneous laughter had lit up a dark room inside her. She hadn't realized before this very moment that the lights had been off.

Joe pulled the collar up on his fleece-lined jacket and adjusted his Stetson as the chilled air hit his neck. He turned his head and took in the silhouette of the Sangre de Cristo Mountains, then spared a quick glance over his shoulder.

"I'm still here," Becca called out.

He held back a chuckle and waited for her to catch up. Who would have thought he'd be riding his ranch with Becca? Now wasn't the time to analyze the confusion he felt around her. For the moment, he was simply going to appreciate that it was spring and he was alive.

Yeah, being alive was good. There was a time in Afghanistan when he wondered if he'd ever be back in the saddle. After he'd dropped the tractor on his arm, he wasn't sure if he ever wanted to be. Life as a one-armed rancher was more challenging than he cared to admit. He'd like to be able to say he'd moved on. But that wouldn't happen until the prosthesis was paid for and he proved he could run his own ranch by himself again. And that meant Becca would be gone.

He wasn't ready to consider why that should give him pause. After all, leaving was probably the only thing he could count on for certain with Becca.

A breeze brushed against his face, teasing him with the scent of spring wildflowers. This was his favorite time of year. The time when the valley woke from winter's slumber and all sorts of surprises peeked out from the soil. The hundreds of spring and late-spring bulbs his mother had planted around the ranch, when she thought he wasn't looking, were blooming. The scent of daffodil, freesia, iris and anemone rode the morning air.

Joe led Blackie along the perimeter of the ranch, keeping to the fence line until they reached the pasture where the cattle currently grazed.

"How many head?" Becca asked.

"About two hundred."

Joe slid from his horse to the ground. He tied the reins to a tree with a slipknot and headed to the water troughs. The dogs dutifully followed him.

"Do you want help?" she asked.

"Nah. They're set to autofill. I'm just checking for contamination." Finding everything in order he mounted Blackie again.

Sunrise continued a steady appearance behind them, as they headed the horses toward the hay fields. Riding slowly near the crop, he began to check the stalks.

"How do you know when it's ready to harvest?" Becca asked.

"Didn't your daddy teach you about hay?"

"No. My father was a cowboy, not a farmer."

"We run a small operation. You have to be both around here." He nodded toward the crop. "Timing is everything. It's as much a fine art as it is a science. We want the young, tender stalks."

"Looks to me like it's about ready, isn't it?"

"Yeah. Almost. This will be the first cutting of the year. That means the highest quality alfalfa hay. The question is, will the hay mature and Mother Nature cooperate at the same time?"

"The hay will make or break your operation?"

"Probably not. We're fortunate to have water rights on the property that bring in a little extra income, though not everyone in Paradise is happy about that situation. But with the high cost of hay, cutting and baling our own is one less expense. Sometimes we even have enough to sell. That would be a very good year."

"So it's all a gamble," she observed.

"You said it. Basically the only thing I can control is the machines. So I'm getting the windrower, rake and bale wagon ready to go."

"What will happen if it rains?" Becca asked.

"If the weather doesn't hold, we'll have to do it sooner than planned, and OrthoBorne will have to wait its turn. All we need is a couple of sunshine days strung together to get the job done."

"Does 'we' mean you?"

"Usually Dan is here. Even then, sometimes we bring in a contractor with his own machine to assist, or an extra ranch hand. It will all depend on the budget. When the weather is fickle, I'm likely to let anyone help."

Sliding off Blackie, he tossed the reins over the saddle and pointed to a four-wire fence. "Need to fix this barbed wire, as it's a little loose. Then we're done."

"I can do that. I've fixed many a fence in my day."

Joe nearly laughed aloud. "In your day, huh? How old are you?"

"Thirty-one." She frowned as she dismounted. "Are you making fun of me?"

"Not at all." He offered her the fence pliers. "I'll let you take care of this, then. I'm going to have a look at that downed tree over there. Probably come back later with the truck and chain saw."

Joe led his horse to the creek, where indeed a tall cottonwood had been struck by lightning. Its twisted trunk was split and lay between the grass and the creek. The dogs followed, running through the long grass that grew near the water, chasing each other.

"Come on, boys. Let's go see if that old cowgirl is done."

Becca was in the saddle and waiting for him as they moved down the fence line. Joe inspected the barbed wire with exaggerated care. "Nicely done," he finally pronounced.

"Thank you." She handed him the pliers.

"Let's get you back before your city slickers show up and get into trouble again."

"I can go back alone," she said.

"No. We ride in pairs around here."

"You're the only one here most of the time."

"Except for me. I'm the boss."

"Overall, how did I do?" Becca asked once they returned to the barn.

"You did two hours of good riding. I imagine that answer will be obvious tomorrow after your city muscles start complaining."

"Faint praise?"

"Not at all. You did fine."

"Fine?" She uttered a noise of displeasure, and as if to agree, Princess snorted. Joe hid his smile. Becca had done more than fine, keeping up with him as he moved along the perimeter of the ranch making note of work that would need to be done later. A tedious chore, but necessary.

"Fine is a good thing. I noticed you didn't mention how I did. You were, after all, observing my daily activities."

"As a horseman, you're far exceeding my expectations. As a rancher, well, that remains to be seen. You still favor your left hand."

"Fair enough," Joe replied. "So I guess I did fine, as well."

Becca shook her head, but said nothing more.

Silence stretched as he rubbed down his horse.

He closed the stall behind Blackie and turned in time to see Becca pull off her gloves and wince.

"You all right?"

"Yes." She tucked the palm of her left hand under her arm. "I cut my hand on the fence wire. It was fine until I yanked my glove off and it started bleeding again. No big deal."

"Those fancy gloves. Why didn't you say something?" he muttered.

"No big deal," she insisted.

"Let me see your hand."

"I'm fine, Joe."

"I need to see your hand." He sucked in a breath when she offered the palm for his inspection. Jaw clamped tight, all he could do was stare at the ragged cut, oozing blood, that marred her smooth skin. His gaze went from her hand to her face as irritation began to build.

"The glove has a cotton liner that clotted the cut. I didn't realize—"

"Your tetanus shot up-to-date?" he fairly snapped.

"Yes."

"First-aid kit is over here." Joe moved to the other side of the barn where he'd built counters for working on paperwork. He pulled open a cabinet and yanked out the large first-aid kit.

"That's some kit," she murmured.

"My brother is a pharmacist and my sister-in-law is a doctor. They keep it well stocked." He tucked a bottle of sterile water under his arm and opened it with his left hand. "Here, slosh this over the cut. Use the whole bottle."

While she complied, he tore open sterile gauze packs with his teeth.

"You can use your prosthetic fingers to hold the gauze squares while you tear the package open."

Joe slowly lifted his head to meet her gaze. "Seriously? You're going to give me a lesson...*now*?"

"I said we'd being doing teaching in the field. The more you make yourself use the prosthesis, the more second nature it will become. If you keep accommodating and ignoring the device, then your myoelectric prosthesis is really just an expensive toy."

He took a deep breath. "Duly noted."

She nodded and took the gauze from him.

"Let me get the antibiotic ointment," Joe said. He pulled the tube from the kit and looked from her to the cap. Determined to use his right hand, he focused on utilizing his muscles to generate the movement that allowed him to grasp the tube. Then, using his left hand, he removed the lid.

"Nicely done," Becca murmured with her eyes on the tube and his prosthesis. She took the tube from him and applied a blob of clear ointment to her laceration line before topping it with the gauze. "Tape?" she asked.

"I've got wrapping gauze. That'll work better with your glove."

Joe held the small roll of gauze with his prosthetic hand and tore off the paper before handing it to her.

"Um, you'll have to hold it in place while I wrap," Becca said. Her lips curved in a small smile at the irony of the situation.

Yeah. He got it. *They both were handicapped now.*

Stepping closer, Joe held the end of the gauze against her skin. He averted his gaze, refusing to consider how soft her skin was or how long it had been they'd been this close. A lifetime ago, and the memories were as vivid today as then.

His gaze traveled from her jaunty ponytail sticking out of the back of the ball cap to the curve of her jaw as she concentrated.

Becca wrapped the roll around her palm several times, tucking the ends under. When she finished, she raised her head and their eyes met. She froze and licked her lips. "I… I…"

"All set?" Joe asked, stepping back into his safety zone.

"Yes. Thank you."

He could only grunt a response.

"Joe?" Becca said his name softly. Barely a whisper as it slid over him.

He raised his brows in question.

"I'm so sorry." Her eyes were sincere as she pleaded with him.

Sorry? She was twelve years too late for sorry. He turned and headed out of the barn, cautioning himself. He had vowed not to make the same mistake again. If he did, he'd be twice the fool.

Chapter Five

Rebecca poured coffee into a to-go cup and rummaged around in the darkened kitchen for a lid. When the lights suddenly came on, she was blinded and nearly stumbled over a chair.

"Mom? I sure hope that's you."

She heard a familiar chuckle and turned to see her mother tighten the belt on her old, blue chenille robe.

"Yes. Of course it's me. Sorry. Did I startle you?"

"That you did. It's four in the morning. What are you doing up?"

"I've hardly seen you this week. Goodness, you've put in long hours at the Gallagher Ranch."

"Oh, Mom. I'm sorry. You shouldn't have to get up at four to see your daughter. Things will slow down soon."

"All the same, this is what mothers do when they're looking for an opportunity to say they're extremely proud of their children."

"Aw, thank you." Rebecca popped two slices of oat nut bread into the toaster. "But here I proclaim my independence and then turn around only to ask you more favors. I appreciate you helping with Casey during the week."

"She's my granddaughter. I'm happy to. We'll manage

around Casey's summer vacation." Joan opened the cupboard and grabbed a large container of peanut butter. She slid the jar across the laminate countertop to Rebecca.

"I only wish I could tell you what time I'll be home today."

"No worries. This brings back memories of you and your father putting in sixteen-hour days on Elliott Ranch."

"Yes. You are so right." Rebecca grinned. "Those are wonderful memories, too. I loved working with Dad."

"Did you ever think you'd be on a ranch again?"

"No. I thought my ranch days were long gone once we lost Dad."

Joan shook her head. "Well, just like the good old days, you have to go out even in lousy weather. Take my rain slicker, will you? It's pouring out there."

"Thanks, Mom." Rebecca pulled a butter knife from the drawer.

"When are you moving into the cottage?"

"Casey's last day of school is today, so maybe tonight. Maybe tomorrow. Are you sure you're okay with watching Casey while I'm working?"

"I'm happy to. It means less disruption in her life. We'll all work around your crazy schedule."

"Thank you." Rebecca smiled, her gaze fixed on the glowing grates of the toaster. Her chest ached with joy, just thinking about the little house. "I keep pinching myself because it's so perfect. Two bedrooms. A small, but modern kitchen with all the amenities. The house is furnished, too. Did I mention that?"

"No. That's wonderful."

The browned bread popped up, and she plucked the slices from the toaster. "Oh, and there are clay pots outside that are begging for summer flowers."

"Casey is going to love helping you plant."

"That's exactly what I thought." Rebecca unscrewed the lid of the peanut butter jar. "I know it's only for a short time, but living a normal life again is all I ever dreamed about when the trial was going on."

"Oh, Becca." Her mother closed the distance between them, wrapping her in a hug. Releasing Rebecca, she hesitated for a moment before taking a deep breath. "Honey, there was something else I wanted to discuss with you before you leave."

Rebecca stiffened, sensing the uneasy tone in her mother's voice. "Is everything okay?"

She nodded. "I, um, I got an email from Casey's other grandmother."

"Virginia emailed you?"

"Apparently the family is back in Four Forks for the summer. Nick's sister is graduating from college. On Sunday. They want Casey to attend a party. Though it is short notice."

"Jana graduating. Oh my. It seems like just yesterday that she was the youngest bridesmaid at my wedding."

"Yes. Time does race by, doesn't it?" her mother mused.

Rebecca nodded. "You were worried about telling me about this?"

"Not worried. I've tried to banish that word from my vocabulary and turn things over to God. Yet try as I might, I can't help but be concerned. You know Judge Brown will be there."

"The judge and I may have our issues, but Casey should still have the advantage of growing up with her extended family."

"You aren't concerned about the judge?"

"Of course I am, but I'm still going to try to do the

right thing. I'm believing Virginia has my back this time, as well."

"Then why didn't she do something when you were arrested? All those ridiculous accusations that she knew weren't true."

"Mom, I've told you before. Virginia Simpson isn't like you or me. She's been taken care of all her life. That doesn't make her a bad person." She sighed and shook her head. "Besides, it wasn't her job to defend me against her father. In the end it was God's job."

"You're a much nicer person than I am, Rebecca."

"Don't give me too much credit."

"You're going to let Casey attend?"

"If that's what she wants."

"I could drop her off, if that will help you. I have plans, and it's right on my way. Virginia did mention she'd be happy to bring Casey home."

"That's probably the best arrangement. Thank you for offering, Mom."

"Thank you for reminding me to be more charitable."

Rebecca glanced at the wall clock. "Uh-oh, I have to shower and get dressed."

"You didn't eat your toast."

Rebecca reached for a small plate. "I'll eat while I'm getting ready."

"Some things never change."

"You're remembering high school, right? Always on the run."

"Exactly." Her mother paused for a moment. "Rebecca?"

"Mmm."

"Isn't it awkward working with Joe Gallagher?"

"Challenging. That's what it is."

"Do you ever wonder...?"

Rebecca's head jerked up in time to meet her mother's wistful gaze. "No. Let's not go there."

"Does that mean you *do* wonder?" her mother murmured with a small smile.

"Mom, to tell you the truth, I can't allow myself to think about anything. I've made wrong choices in my life. I don't know if I trust my judgment anymore."

"Don't blame yourself because you believed in the good in people."

"I do blame myself." She took a deep breath. "I'm grateful the Lord kept his hand on Casey the entire time."

"We're only human, Rebecca. Sometimes all you can do is ask for forgiveness before moving on."

"I'm grateful He forgives."

"That doesn't mean you should shut yourself off from the possibility of finding happiness."

"I'm not. I'm just not looking for anything beyond what the Lord has given me today. One step at a time is about all I can handle."

"Rain." Joe grimaced and stared out the kitchen window at the gray world outside. Fat drops plopped onto the gravel drive and the yard, creating muddy puddles. Overhead, thunder cracked, promising continued rain. Another dismal and bleak day, guaranteed to leave him soaking wet and chilled to the core.

He lifted a mug to his lips. Even the aroma of strong, rich coffee and Patti Jo's muffins waiting on a platter couldn't lift his sour mood.

Truth be told, he'd like to have words with that smiley-faced meteorologist on television. The man was obviously not familiar with ranches. If he were, he'd use caution before sharing his weather promises for Paradise and the valley.

Scattered rain showers? Twenty-four hours of solid

rain, hammering down, was what he should have announced.

Joe shook his head. Nothing to be done about the situation. Becca's smile was pretty much the only thing positive about the last few days, though he sure wasn't going to tell her that.

She'd been upbeat despite the weather, taking the crew to town yesterday for a tour of the historic landmarks in downtown Paradise, which took all of fifteen minutes. They'd stopped for lunch, and Becca brought him back a box of his favorite muffins from Patti Jo's. A gruff thank you was all he could muster at the time. Fact was, he was floored she remembered that he preferred blueberry muffins.

If she was trying to test him, she was doing a good job.

He kept reminding himself that there wasn't a single reason to strike up anything but a business relationship with the woman. It may have been twelve years ago, but he had nothing more to offer her now than he did then. It was more than apparent in hindsight that back then his future on Gallagher Ranch wasn't enough to keep her in Paradise.

Not a thing had changed in the years since. He remained a rancher who was getting by. Not a rich successful lawyer like her husband had been.

Besides, she'd sign off on his certification and be gone again in a month or so. No, he'd continue to keep her at a distance. It was better for everyone.

Joe checked the fit on his hook prosthesis. The myoelectric version wasn't waterproof, and rain or no rain, he had work that couldn't wait another day.

When he opened the front door, once again, Becca stood outside. This time she wore a cheery yellow hooded rain slicker over blue jeans. Her head was turned up toward the sky like a kid, letting the drops kiss her face.

"What are you doing?" he growled.

"I like rain. Don't you?" Drops of moisture clung to her long black lashes. She pushed a wayward lock of dark hair into the hood of the slicker, waiting for his response.

Joe stared, entranced, as the rain moved leisurely down her face, landing on her lips.

"Joe?"

He blinked. "Yeah. I like rain, too. In moderation. I like everything in moderation," he muttered. "I keep whispering that word into Mother Nature's ear, except she's deaf." Slapping on his Stetson, he tucked his face into the collar of his coat and strode across the yard. Today he was headed to the equipment garage.

"What will you do if it keeps raining?"

"Watch and wait. Just another day in Paradise." He dodged a puddle and turned to her. "What are you doing here so early, anyhow? Not much for you or your crew to do today."

"I need to talk to you about the photo shoot."

"What photo shoot? It's raining."

She grimaced. "Yes. It's been raining for twenty-four hours. This is Friday, and the crew is getting antsy. Rod suggested, um well, they, ah… They want to do some filming in the barn with the horses and the dogs and hay and such."

He pulled open the big door to the garage and held it for her.

Becca nodded her thanks. "They've been very patient, and I…that is…I think they've acclimated to the ranch well, don't you?"

"You mean that guy who keeps complaining about a rash?"

"Poison oak. Yes. That would be Julian. Even he's adjusting well, since I got him some cortisone cream. I bet you hardly noticed them following you around the stalls yesterday morning, right?"

Joe snickered. Unable to hold back, he began to belly laugh.

"What's so funny?"

"Becca, it's a little hard not to notice three city folks stumbling around in the dark at five in the morning, crinkling food wrappers and whispering. They spooked Blackie when the alarm clock on somebody's cell phone went off, and then one of them stepped on Wishbone's tail."

"That was an accident. It could have happened to anyone."

"It never happened to you."

"Be fair. I was raised on a ranch. These are people whose idea of roughing it would be coffee in a foam cup."

Joe offered only a snort to that. He flipped on the overhead lights. "I don't even understand why they were there yesterday. Nothing for them to do when it's raining."

"They need to get to know you and your routine. That's what will make this project a success." She paused. "Rod spent yesterday afternoon sketching plans for the shoot and checking lighting and set design with Julian."

Joe pulled back the riding lawn mower and unscrewed the oil cap. Today would be a fine day to check on the mowers and replace that part that came in on the baler, he thought. Pulling out the dipstick, he wiped it off on a clean rag.

Becca stepped closer, her muddy boots inches away from his. He kept his focus on the dipstick measurement and inched back from her.

"Are you listening to me?"

He looked up. "Sure am. Hard not to when you're in my face."

She ignored his remark and continued. "Abi's fitting in pretty well, isn't she?" she asked.

"Yeah, okay, yes. Abi has been the least obnoxious of the group." Joe released what he hoped was a long-suffering sigh. "What do you have in mind for the photo shoot?"

"Rod asked for a couple of hours. Maybe this afternoon after lunch?"

"I've got a few calls to make. How about two?"

"Sure. He wants you to bring a few of your Western dress shirts. Pearl button. And maybe a bolo tie. Oh, and wear your Tony Llamas, not work boots. He'd like you to bring both your tan and your black Stetsons and your straw Resistol."

"How does he know I have a straw Resistol?" He crouched a bit lower to examine the blade on the mower.

She cleared her throat. "I might have mentioned that I saw it on a coatrack at your house."

"Anything else?"

"Yes, Abi needs to do a one-on-one interview with you. This might be a good opportunity," she said with a hopeful tone.

"Fine," he said through gritted teeth. "Point me in the right direction at the right time, and I'll do whatever we need to do to get them out of here quickly."

"Two it is. I'll have them set up and meet you in the barn."

"Fine. Whatever." He reached for a can of oil. "What are you going to do until then?"

"I'll drive back to town," she said. "Unless you'd like to squeeze in a therapy session while you work on the equipment."

"What?" The wrench slipped from his fingers and clanged as it hit the mower and tumbled to the ground. He scowled, his gaze on the tool. "No. I really need to get some work done today."

"Fine. Then I'll see you after lunch. Oh, and I appreciate your cheerful attitude, Mr. Gallagher. It makes my job so much easier."

Joe tipped his hat back, his gaze following her as she offered him a two-fingered salute and then turned on her heel, making it clear that her determination to get the job done would outlast his bad attitude.

"Rod, you're amazing." Rebecca glanced around the main area of the barn. Round bales of hay had been strategically stacked and placed in the center. A seating area had been created from single hay bundles. Lights hung from the ceiling on a rope of orange industrial extension cords, and reflector boards were propped and ready for use.

"What time did you get here?" she asked.

"Two hours ago," Julian said. "He wouldn't even let me order a second piece of caramel apple pie at Patti Jo's."

Rod held a fancy camera in the air as he took an exaggerated bow in response to her compliment.

"Too bad we can't do something about that smell," Julian commented.

"What smell?" Rebecca asked.

"That horse manure." Julian shivered and shook his head. "Ugh, it's thick today."

Rebecca laughed. "This is a barn. I should warn you two that there's no guarantee the horses won't decide to mess up your shoot, if you know what I mean."

"Terrific," Rod said drily. He looked to Julian. "Let's

save the horses for our outdoor shoot. We'll use the dogs instead."

Abi stepped into the barn, peeled off her wet jacket and evaluated the area. "Nice work, guys!" She leaned close to Rebecca. "I'm guessing your cowboy isn't going to be real happy about doing this in the middle of his workday."

"He isn't my cowboy."

The smiling journalist shrugged. "I call 'em as I see 'em. When you're in the vicinity, Mr. Gallagher only has eyes for you."

"That's because he's looking for another opportunity to bite off my head."

"I don't think so," Abi said in a singsongy voice.

From behind them, Joe Gallagher cleared his throat.

Rebecca whirled around.

Looking handsome enough to take her breath away, the rancher stood in the doorway of the barn, closing a huge black umbrella. He wore creased Levi's and a crisp white pearl-button Western shirt. His black hair was damp and curled slightly over his ears. And he'd shaved. Rebecca couldn't even remember the last time she'd seen the man clean shaven. She examined the smooth planes of his angular face and found no evidence that he'd nicked himself.

"What are you looking at?" Joe asked.

"You mentioned losing a pint of blood when you shave," Rebecca murmured.

"I've been practicing," he returned.

"So I see."

He held a white straw Resistol and his Stetsons stacked in one hand. A spare shirt on a hanger dangled from his prosthetic fingers as his gaze swept across the impromptu photography setup.

"You certainly clean up nicely," Abi drawled, as she took the shirt and hats from Joe.

He responded with a wink and a wide, winning smile that made even the sassy journalist blush.

It was clear to everyone in the room why this particular cowboy had been chosen for the advertising campaign. He was definitely the perfect poster boy for OrthoBorne, despite his numerous protests.

It was also obvious that Abi had been plain wrong in her summation of where Joe's interests were. It had been a good twelve years since Joe had offered a smile like that to Rebecca.

"Julian," Rod called out. "We're ready for makeup."

"Makeup?" Joe stepped back and held up a palm. "Whoa."

"It's a loose powder that absorbs oil. We apply it with a sponge to keep your skin from shining under the lights."

"Makeup." Joe repeated the word on a sour note.

Julian inched nervously toward his model. "Could you sit down?"

Joe averted his gaze, as though wishing himself elsewhere, and eased down to a bale of hay.

"Close your eyes, please."

The cowboy tightened his jaw when Julian dabbed the powder on his face.

All Rebecca could do was cringe, praying Julian would finish quickly.

"Now let's get you comfortable," Rod said. "Go ahead and lean back against the hay." He moved in to position Joe's arm.

Not a thing about Joe looked comfortable. Rebecca started nibbling on her thumbnail.

"Julian, get that light over here. Abi, do you mind

holding the silver reflector board for me?" Rod nodded and pulled out a light meter. "Higher please."

"Chin up, Joe. Give us a smile, like the love of your life walked into the room."

Joe's eyes widened and his gaze locked with Rebecca's. His lips curled dangerously. She met his eyes, straight on and worked hard not to flinch. No, she wouldn't back down.

"Rebecca. Your phone," Abi whispered.

"I'm sorry. Excuse me. I'll step outside." She pulled up the hood on her slicker and ducked out to the yard to check the number. *Unidentified*.

"Hello?"

The call disconnected, and she stood staring at the device. Could it have been her mother from an outside number? She scrolled through and found the familiar number. "Hey, Mom. Just checking to be sure you weren't trying to reach me… Okay, great. I'll talk to you later. I should be done here early." She stepped into the barn in time to hear Joe arguing with Julian.

"Touch my hat, and I might have to relocate your fingers."

Julian jumped back. "But Rod said to adjust the brim."

"Do you have a mirror?" Rebecca asked, intervening.

"Sure," Rod said. He rummaged in a large duffel and passed a hand mirror to her.

"Okay, Rod," Rebecca said. "Can you tell Mr. Gallagher how you want the Resistol?"

"Push back those curls in front and put the hat on the back of your head. Sort of rakish."

"Rakish?" Joe repeated.

"Yeah. Like a bad boy."

"A bad boy," Joe muttered the words and adjusted the hat.

"Perfect. Now turn slightly to the left, chin up."

Joe stiffly complied.

"You don't happen to have a guitar, do you?" Rod asked.

This time Joe's brows rose.

"I guess that's a no." Rod glanced around. "Becca, can you get that rope from the tack room? The one that was hanging from the horse."

She raced to grab the coiled lasso rope from the wall.

"Perfect. Okay, try this. Hold that rope with your prosthesis. Let it rest against your leg."

Again Joe complied, his green eyes dark and annoyed.

"Stretch your legs out in front of you and cross them at the ankles, so we get the boots in the picture." Rod kept circling around Joe and the bales of hay, snapping dozens of pictures. Finally he paused to evaluate. "Nice."

"Does that mean we're done?" Joe began to rise.

"No. Sit. Head down. Turn right, and tip the brim of your hat over your face. Let your prosthesis rest on your bent knee."

The tension in the barn was palpable as Rod continued to call out orders and snap digital pictures.

"*Julian.* He's shiny on the right side."

Julian stepped hesitantly toward Joe with a powder sponge.

"Rebecca," Rod called out. "We need a saddle. And the dogs. Where are the dogs?"

Joe whistled for Gil and Wishbone, while Rebecca strode back to the tack room and grabbed a saddle from the wall.

"Toss it over that high bale of hay behind Mr. Gallagher."

She slung the saddle awkwardly and missed, nearly

hitting the dogs. Joe stood and easily scooped the leather from her hands and lifted it into place.

"Thank you."

"I'm about two hands shy of fed up," he murmured, his breath warm against her ear.

Startled, she met his gaze. "We're almost done."

Joe dutifully returned to his position against the hay, and Rod began adjusting the reflector board.

"Can you make the dogs sit still?" Rod asked.

"Sit." Joe bellowed the command. The dogs sat, as did Jullan.

"What's that smell?" Abi whispered to Rebecca.

Rebecca glanced around. "It does smell funny, doesn't it?"

Rod looked at Joe. "Do you mind changing into another shirt and grabbing the black Stetson?

A cell phone began to ring.

Joe pulled it from his back pocket. "Yeah, Jake. Sure. I'll be there in a bit. Thanks."

"Everything okay?" Rebecca asked.

"The other piece for the windrower is in. I'll need to get to town."

"We're almost done here," Rod said.

"Jake closes early on Friday," Joe stated.

Rod looked from Joe to Rebecca. She nodded her agreement with Joe.

"Okay," Rod said. "I'll look over today's shots. Hopefully we have something to work with."

"What about my interview?" Abi asked.

"Talk to Becca," Joe said. Pausing, he glanced around the barn. "Something is burning."

He strode to the wall and grabbed the fire extinguisher before searching the barn, stall by stall. Rebecca followed.

Joe stopped suddenly at a wall outlet. His wide shoulders heaved, and he let out a frustrated breath before yanking out two heavy-duty extension cords piggybacked into the wall outlet.

The overhead lights went dark.

"They could have burned down my barn," Joe fairly growled. He whipped around. Face thunderous, he pinned her with an icy glare. "They could have burned down my barn, Becca."

"I'm sorry, Joe. This is my fault. Rod and Julian got here before me and set up."

"You're right, it is your fault. I'm trying to save my ranch, and this is the second time they've fouled things up."

"It won't happen again."

"It can't happen again." He took a deep breath as if willing himself to calm down. Then he met her gaze. "Becca, life as a one-armed rancher is more challenging than I'd ever admit to anyone. Except maybe you. All I want to do is move on. But that can't happen until the prosthesis is paid for and life returns to normal. I'm willing to do whatever it takes, but my patience is running thin."

She bit her lip and nodded. "I'm sorry, Joe. It seems that all I can offer is another apology, and I realize that doesn't cut it."

Joe massaged his forehead with his fingers. "When are you moving into the cottage?"

"Tomorrow."

"Good. This isn't going to work unless you can ride herd on this team."

"You have my word."

"I'm counting on you, Becca. Gallagher Ranch is counting on you."

Rebecca swallowed. The man certainly knew how to

hit her right where her guilt was located. He was right. So far her attempts to get this project on track were failing miserably. If Joe failed, she failed, as well. It was time to step up her game. Both their futures were on the line.

Chapter Six

"**W**ho's that?" Casey asked.

Rebecca pulled on the Honda's parking brake. She looked from her daughter in the passenger seat, staring glumly out the car window, to Joe Gallagher, who stood in front of their new home. The cowboy's arms were crossed, his prosthesis visible in a black short-sleeve T-shirt. His face was unreadable as he watched the packed Honda edge up the circular gravel drive.

Why was Joe here? He should be off doing whatever it was he did on Saturday afternoons.

"That's Mr. Gallagher. Remember, I told you that this is his ranch."

"Why is he mad?"

Rebecca sucked in a breath. "He's not mad."

"He looks mad to me."

"No. He's just frowning. Joe, I mean, Mr. Gallagher, does that when he's nervous."

"Why is he nervous?"

"You know what? I think he might be a little scared to meet you, sweetie."

Casey unbuckled her seat belt and turned, her gaze

meeting her mother's. Her brown eyes rounded beneath the fringe of chocolate-brown bangs. "Me?"

Rebecca nodded. "I told him how awesome you are. Come to think of it, he may be a little scared you won't like him."

Her daughter's small mouth formed a perfect little circle of astonishment.

"We better get moving, Case. We have a lot of work to do." Rebecca glanced at the backseat. "Why don't you start by grabbing your suitcase? Then you can work on those smaller boxes with your name on them. Take them right to your room. Okay?"

"Okay, Momma, but, how do I know which room is mine?"

"Yours is the pink one, of course."

"I have a pink room?" She beamed, pleasure lighting up her face.

"That's what Mr. Gallagher told me." Rebecca opened her car door and popped the trunk. "We can move all the boxes in before we begin to unpack."

Joe moved down the steps toward them. "I thought you might need some help."

"How did you know we were here?"

"I was on my way over to make sure everything was turned on."

"Thank you. We don't want to take you away from your work."

"Paperwork today. It can wait."

She nodded and narrowed her eyes at him. "I don't suppose you happen to know how to smile?"

"Excuse me?"

She narrowed her eyes. "Casey thinks you're mad at her."

"Me?" He blinked with surprise. "You can't be serious."

"I'm very serious. You look a little intimidating with that expression on your face and that black getup."

"What are you talking about?" He glanced down at his black jeans and black shirt.

"You're making a six-year-old nervous."

"Are you messing with me?" He took off his black ball cap and slapped it back on. "I have a niece, and she's not afraid of me. Kids usually like me."

"Casey isn't like most kids."

He hesitated for a moment. "Did you tell her about my arm? Maybe that's what's scaring her."

Rebecca glanced at his arm. "Why would I?" she returned. "And she distinctly asked why you were mad. She doesn't care about your prosthesis."

"I don't know..." His chin was set as he uttered the words.

"Joe, you are not defined by your residual limb. No one cares. It's not as big a deal to everyone else as it is to you."

He gave a slow nod as though considering her words. Then he strode over to the car and held the back door for Casey, who struggled with a suitcase.

"May I help you with that, ma'am?"

Startled, Casey jumped. She looked him up and down. "Okay," she said softly.

"I'm Joe."

"I'm Casey."

"Nice to meet you," he said.

She glanced from his face to his prosthesis and then nodded. "Cool arm."

"Uh, thanks."

Rebecca passed by him with a box tucked under her chin. "Told you so," she murmured.

Joe put the suitcase on the front walk, shook his head and went back to the trunk for another box.

"Is this all you have?" he asked as he followed Rebecca into the house.

"There's two more boxes in the front seat."

"That's not much. Where's all your other stuff? No U-Haul or anything?"

"There is no other stuff." She chuckled. "I am probably the only woman you will ever meet with a lot of baggage but without a lot of stuff."

He opened his mouth, then pressed his lips together, brows knit.

"What?" she asked.

"Not a thing." He raised a palm in defense.

"You know you want to ask, so I may as well tell you." She glanced around to be sure Casey was out of earshot. "I sold pretty much everything I owned to pay for the attorney fees and court costs, and to keep us solvent when I wasn't employed."

"You were fired, too?"

"Not at all. OrthoBorne held my job when I took a leave of absence. It was difficult to work when the accident and the trial were regularly in the news. Of course, it didn't take long to burn through my vacation and sick time, either."

"Didn't Nick have a life insurance policy or savings account or something?"

"He sure did. Life insurance policy, as well as a hefty savings account. I was unable to access either of them until I was cleared of all charges."

Rebecca put her box down on the floor in the living room, and Joe followed suit.

"The legal system frowns on handing out money to murderers. By the time I had access to any resources, it was much too late. I used those funds to pay my attorney and the staggering list of bills I had accumulated. The leftover is in the bank for Casey's college education."

Joe ran a hand over his face. "I'm sorry you had to go through all that, Becca. You lost everything, even though you were innocent."

She shrugged. "God's taking care of us."

"How can you be so blasé about what they did to you?"

"Not they. Judge Brown. Yet I am certain that holding on to bitter feelings would only make me exactly like him, so I take it to the Lord when I'm tempted to be resentful. Which, on a bad day, can be often. He said he'd never leave me. He hasn't."

"You think not?" Joe asked.

"I know not." She cocked her head and looked at him. "The old Joe Gallagher wouldn't have doubted Him."

"The old Joe Gallagher. I have no idea who he is, let alone how God fits into things," Joe muttered.

"You'll find Him again, eventually. When you least expect it." She glanced around. "So are you going to give me the tour?" Rebecca asked, glad to change the subject.

"Sure. Sure. Of course."

He moved into the cozy living room where a leather sofa and two leather chairs were positioned in front of a stone fireplace.

Rebecca ran a hand over the back of the couch, imagining a relaxing evening with the fire blazing in the hearth, a quilt on her lap and a book in her hand.

"There are two fireplaces," Joe said. "The other one is in the master bedroom. Firewood is on the back porch. As you may remember, we never know what the weather is going to do in the valley, no matter what month the calendar says it is. We have to be prepared."

"Why did Dan leave this lovely place?"

"Dan and Beth want a big family. They built a larger house near town. She works at the Paradise Hospital, and he's either at the pharmacy in town or at the clinic. It only made sense to live closer to downtown."

Joe moved through the kitchen. "Furnace is in this closet. Instructions are taped on the wall inside." He kept walking and tapped his knuckles on the entrance to a small room near the back of the house. "Washing machine, dryer and hot-water tank are in here." Then he pulled open the back door to reveal a screened-in porch with two red rocking chairs, parked beside a stack of empty terra-cotta planters.

Rebecca released a small gasp as she took in the view. "I can see straight to the mountains."

Joe turned to follow her gaze to the west. "Pretty spectacular. I guess I take it for granted. It's good to see my world through someone else's eyes."

"There's still snow on the Sangre de Christos."

"Yeah, it's been a chilly spring."

"A garden patch." She peered through the screen into the yard. The grass was freshly mowed, the garden recently tilled. Neat rows of soil begged for planting. Beyond the garden, the lawn stretched to a grouping of conifers on the right, and behind them, a fence indicated the border of Gallagher Ranch.

"Yeah, I guess so. Small one. Beth, Dan's wife, grew vegetables. I forgot about that."

Rebecca lowered herself to one of the rocking chairs and set it to a slow rhythmic motion with her foot. Planting a garden would be like setting down roots. But where would she be when it was harvest time? It seemed almost cruel to tempt her with the thought. She probably wasn't even going to have time to plant the flowers in those big pots and planters, the way things were moving along.

Suddenly realization hit her. She stopped the movement of the rocker and looked up at Joe. "I need to give you a deposit."

"Huh?"

"A deposit. On the cottage."

"No."

"Let me know what day you prefer that I turn in the rent. I know we haven't discussed this, but I'm hoping you charge about the same as the house I was going to lease. I'm happy to pay you weekly, since I don't know how long I'll be here."

"I'm not charging rent." The words were flat, laced with the usual Joe Gallagher high and mighty annoyance.

Rebecca stood. "Give me a good reason why not."

Joe leaned against the doorjamb, his arms crossed in a take-no-prisoners stance. "First of all, my mother would kill me if she found out. Second, you're going to help me with the media crew. And third, it's not my house. When Dan gave me the keys, he told me to use it if I get a ranch hand."

"Then I shouldn't be staying here." She shook her head. "And you shouldn't be offering the place."

"If I get a ranch hand, it'll only be for a week or so during the hay harvest. He can stay at my place. That's the way we've always done things in the past."

"I don't do charity." She met his gaze. "Period."

"This isn't charity. Charity is what they do down at the Paradise Valley Church. If you want to throw money at me, well, I suggest that you put it in the offering plate instead."

Rebecca rubbed the bridge of her nose. Clearly the man was even more stubborn than she was.

"Wednesday evening service is at six," he continued. "Sunday morning services are at eight, nine thirty and eleven. Bit of advice. Avoid the eleven o'clock service. While it is the shortest service of the three since Pastor likes to be out for lunch so he can watch the Broncos games, it's also the one Judge Brown attends."

"You sure know a lot about church services for a man who's turned his back on God."

"I'm pretty sure you're only here to handle my prosthesis, not my soul," he shot back.

"Whatever, Joe. I don't want to argue."

Silence stretched for a moment, until Rebecca couldn't stifle a yawn.

"Tired, huh? Good news is you made it through the week."

"And no one was more surprised than you, right?"

"I didn't say that." His words were a little less sharp this time. "But since you mentioned it, you did surprise me. There's no hiding the fact that you were born to ranch life. Your daddy would be proud."

"Thank you." Embarrassed by his praise, Rebecca shifted to professional mode. "Now that I've got a complete understanding of your ADLs, we're going to have to carve out time to work on some techniques I think may help you fully utilize your prosthesis on the ranch."

"Does that mean I might graduate early?"

"I didn't say that."

"A guy can dream."

"I'll be out of your hair before you know it, Joe. I promise."

"I wasn't trying to get rid of you," he said.

"No?" She glanced up at him.

"No. I think you and I work well together."

Rebecca opened her mouth and then closed it again. Before she could answer, he had turned and walked away. She stared at his retreating form, confused and a little terrified. Joe had every reason to be hard and unforgiving with her, given their past. However, this unexpected crack in the formidable cowboy, well, it was much more than she was ready to handle.

"Don't be nice to me, Joe," she whispered. "I don't deserve it."

Joe walked past Casey's room on his way out of the cottage. He stopped and paused in the doorway, giving a small knock on the door frame.

"Is the bedroom okay?" he asked.

Casey whirled around, her dark braids flying. "Oh, yes. I can't believe it's really mine." Her eyes were bright with pleasure as she assessed the canopy bed and small vanity with its matching mirror and chair.

"Glad to hear it."

"Are there…are there any kids around here?" Casey asked, her voice so soft that Joe had to move closer to hear.

"My niece Amy is on the ranch quite a bit of the time, with her grandmother. Right now she's in California."

When Joe reached for the cord and pulled open the blinds, Casey quickly crossed the room. With her nose nearly pressed against the glass, she anxiously peered out.

"See that big house?" Joe asked.

"Uh-huh."

"That's Amy's grandma's house."

"Is Amy's last name the same as yours?" she asked.

"Yes. That's right. Amy Gallagher. Do you know her?"

"She's in my Sunday-school class. Amy is a year older than me."

"I see."

Casey was silent for moments as she continued to take in the view.

"I like the ranch. It's nice here," she finally breathed.

Joe followed her gaze, once again seeing his home through different eyes. The horses grazed in the yard outside their pavilion, tails swishing back and forth, the slight breeze lifting their manes. Gil and Wishbone slept on the grass, bellies up toward the late-afternoon sun.

"Yeah, it is," he answered.

"Can I ride a horse?"

His eyes widened at the question. "Sure. If your mom says it's okay."

"She will. She rides horses, too, you know."

"Yeah. I heard that."

Casey smiled up at him. "Thanks for letting us stay in your house."

"You're welcome."

"I prayed for you."

"Excuse me?" Joe cocked his head. She had his full attention now.

"I prayed for God to bring a friend for my momma. Someone nice, like you, to make her smile again."

Joe swallowed. He was more than touched by Casey's honest admission. There were no words to say in response to the pureness of heart that shone in her dark eyes.

"Do you have anything else in the car?" he asked.

"Two boxes. Kind of small ones."

"Come on. Let's grab them and get you unpacked, so we can see about a horse."

When Casey took his prosthetic hand in her small one and led him out of the pink bedroom, he found himself speechless yet again.

Minutes later, Joe located Becca in the kitchen putting away the few groceries she'd brought with her.

She turned at the sound of his boots on the hardwood

floor. A grin lit up her face. "The first thing I'm going to do is bake a chocolate cake."

"Okay." He said the word slowly, his mind tripping back in time. Chocolate cake and blue ribbons from the fair. He used to drive her to the fair in Monte Vista and Alamosa every year.

"I'm sorry." Her face reddened as though she was remembering the same thing.

The moment was awkward, and he found himself irritated for no good reason. "You apologize a lot," Joe said, more gruffly than he intended.

"The way I see it, I have a lot to be sorry for." The words tripped from her tongue easily and without guile. She cleared her throat. "Was there something you need?"

"Your daughter would like to ride a horse."

"What?" Her head jerked back, and her brown eyes rounded. "Really?" Her voice rose with a tremor of excitement. "Did she tell you that she wants to ride? My Casey wants to ride?"

"Hold on a minute there." He stopped her, confused by what he was hearing. "Are you telling me that Casey has never ridden...*at all*?"

"No. Never."

"Why, that's plain shameful, especially when she's the granddaughter of a ranch man."

"I have no excuse. You're completely right," Becca murmured, her eyes downcast. "Casey's been shuttled back and forth so much between Paradise and Denver. Sometimes I feel like her entire childhood has been on hold since the accident."

"Well, we can sure take care of that. Right now, in fact."

"Now?"

"Sure. How about if she rides double with you? We can take a short ride down to where the cows are grazing."

"I don't want to inconvenience you. I'm sure you have things to do."

"Not at the moment."

Becca clasped her hands together and grinned. "Thank you, then. Casey will love that."

"I'll meet you at the barn."

"Yes. Yes. I'll get Casey into some blue jeans."

Joe nodded. He turned and tucked his head away from her, before she could see him smiling. Why would it be that making Becca and Casey happy warmed his heart? Maybe he shouldn't overthink this, but simply enjoy the moment.

Chapter Seven

"I'm going to ride a real horse," Casey repeated the words for the umpteenth time as she twirled around the living room.

"Come on, little cowgirl," Rebecca called as she held open the door.

"I'm going to ride a real horse."

"You're going to ride with me," Rebecca said.

"When can I ride by myself?"

"I don't know. These are Mr. Gallagher's horses and—"

"Joe. He said to call him Joe."

"Joe. Yes. Okay. Well, Case, these are Joe's horses and we are here on his ranch. My job comes before riding horses." Rebecca pointed to the barn. "This way."

"Are you doing therapy with Joe?"

"Yes, I am, but remember what I told you. That's confidential. We do not discuss Momma's clients. Ever."

Casey gave a solemn nod. Suddenly her little six-year-old legs picked up speed, the pink sneakers kicking dust into the air as she moved. "There he is. There's Joe. He has the horses."

Rebecca looked straight ahead to where Joe stood in

front of the barn, holding the reins to the gelding and the mare. They were saddled and ready to go.

"Are these ponies?" Casey asked him.

"Ponies?" he scoffed. "These are horses."

"They look like ponies," Casey said.

"Nope." He gave a slow shake of his head. "We measure horses by hands, and these are not ponies."

When Casey screwed up her face, Rebecca nearly laughed out loud.

"I'm serious here," Joe said. "One hand is four inches. We measure from the ground to the top of the withers."

Casey started giggling. "A wither? Wither what?"

Joe chuckled at her response. "This bony part." He ran a hand over Blackie's spine. "This is the wither."

"Can I touch the wither?"

"Sure." Joe scooped her up with his left arm and held her next to the gelding. "Right. There."

"Oh, it is bony," Casey declared with awe as her small hand patted the horse's neck.

"Yep." He let her down again. "Blackie here is sixty-three inches tall or almost sixteen hands. Ponies are anything under fourteen hands and two inches. No ponies on Gallagher Ranch. Not a one."

"Wait until I tell my math teacher about that."

"Higher mathematics," Joe said with a grin for Casey.

It was a killer smile, one that reached his eyes and made Rebecca wish that she had such an easy relationship with the cowboy. She used to. A long time ago.

"Why does he keep moving his tail?" Casey asked.

"That's his flyswatter."

Casey whooped with laughter.

Rebecca stood amazed as the two of them chatted back and forth. He wasn't kidding. Kids did like him.

"Ready?" Joe asked.

"Hmm?" Rebecca returned, her gaze meeting his.

"Casey is ready to ride. How about you?"

"Yes. Of course." Her phone began to ring. When she pulled it out of her back pocket, the unidentified caller hung up. Rebecca shook her head.

"What's wrong?"

"I'm getting hang-up calls," she said quietly, for his ears only.

"Can you tell who it's from?"

"No. I tried that callback method. But whoever it is either has the wrong number or a poor sense of humor."

"How many times have they called?" Joe asked, genuine concern on his face.

"Six times in the last two days."

"*Six*? That's harassment. I can ask Sam what he suggests."

"No. Please don't. I'll contact the sheriff myself if it becomes necessary."

"I don't like it, Becca."

"Neither do I." She turned to Casey. "Ready, sweetie?"

With her daughter's enthusiastic nod of approval, she lifted herself to the saddle and nodded to Joe, who lifted Casey to Rebecca's waiting arms.

"Okay, sit back against me and you hold the reins," Rebecca said.

"Reins?"

Rebecca raised the leather leads. "These help us direct the horse."

"The horse doesn't know his left hand from his right," Joe added as he mounted Blackie.

"Horses have hoofs, not hands." Casey's laughter bubbled over at the words, her gaze upon Joe in a gesture Rebecca recognized as pure hero worship. Mixed emotions settled on Rebecca. It was wonderful for her daughter to have a male role model in her life, but what would happen when the assignment was over and Joe Gallagher no longer welcomed them in his world?

They rode in silence for several minutes until they reached a pasture filled with cows, to the east of the barn.

"Whose cows are those?" Casey asked.

"All mine," Joe returned. "They're eating the grass here until early next week, then I'll move them to another pasture."

"How many head did you say you have?" Rebecca asked.

"Close to two hundred."

"You're going to move two hundred head by yourself?"

"Naw. Gil and Wishbone will help me."

"You can't be serious?"

"Dan usually helps, or my mother."

"Your mother?" Rebecca looked to see if it was a joke. "Elsie really helps you herd cattle?"

"Are you kidding? It was just her and my dad when they started this operation. She'd put Dan and me and my sisters in the pickup truck, which was new back then, and ride along with my father, getting out every now and again when the cows went astray."

"That's amazing."

"That's ranch life," Joe said. "You lived on Elliott Ranch, where the deer and the antelope play and the cash is in abundance."

"It wasn't easy street. We worked sixteen-hour days there, too."

"If you say so."

She cleared her throat, swallowing a lump of hesitation since he was in such a good mood. "Um, I'm happy to help you herd the cattle."

"You?" He turned his head and adjusted his Stetson.

"Yes, me. I've done it before. Many times."

"Who's going to watch the greenhorns if you help me?"

"Couldn't they use the truck and shoot video? We'd be taking care of two things at once." She smiled, pleased at her solution. It was a brilliant plan.

"Might work. Let me think on it."

Rebecca nodded. "Of course." She led Princess away from the fence and followed Blackie as Joe led the horse back toward the ranch.

"What's that?" Casey asked as they neared the corral once more.

Joe and Rebecca both turned to follow Casey's pointing finger. A plastic cow head, complete with horns, was fastened to a round bale of hay, the size of a small heifer.

"Why, that's a dummy steer," Joe said.

"What do you use a dummy for?" Casey's face was bright with amusement, and she seemed about to burst into laughter again.

"I'm learning to rope again with my prosthetic hand. Roping is when you take your rope and twirl it in the air and it lands around the cow. The dummy is how I practice."

"Are you really roping again?" Rebecca asked. "And using your right hand or your left hand?"

"A little of both, and learning is the key word here. I don't have a lot of time right now, but yeah. That's the plan."

"I used to rope," Rebecca mused.

"Give it a shot," Joe said.

"Give what a shot?"

He inclined his head toward the dummy steer.

"Yes, Momma. Do it," Casey urged.

"I don't know."

"Sounds to me like you're changing your story," Joe said.

She turned to him. "It's been a long time."

"You're riding just fine, and you said you can herd cattle." He shrugged. "Try roping on the ground."

"Oh, no. If I'm going to do it, I'm going to do it in the saddle."

"That might be a little ambitious until you develop a feel for the rope again. Those muscles get rusty after…" He cleared his throat. "Twelve years."

"Are you challenging me?"

"That would be foolish. While I have been known to be foolish upon occasion, I would never do anything that might endanger the animals."

"Endanger the animals?" Rebecca huffed. "Casey, honey, I'm going to ease you to the ground. You go sit against the corral fence, and cheer for Momma." As Casey's sneakers hit the dusty earth, Rebecca turned and narrowed her eyes at Joe. "I trust I can borrow your rope."

Joe slowly released the long rope from the pommel and stepped forward with Blackie, handing it over.

"Is it soft enough for you?" Joe asked.

"Just fine."

"You want my gloves? Don't want to burn those pretty hands."

With a death glare shot toward the cowboy, Rebecca yanked her own gloves from her vest pocket. Pretty hands? They were a mess. Torn cuticles and red knuckles along with a healing wire cut in her palm. She tucked her hands into the leather gloves.

Rebecca checked the coils, the loop and the knot. Then she eyed the dummy and began to roll her loop, leading with her thumb and index finger. Yes. She could do this. It was all coming back to her now. Time to throw her catch. The rope sailed underneath the right horn and missed the left horn. Caught off guard, the rope slipped from her hands to the dirt.

"If you did that on the ground, you wouldn't have to keep dismounting," Joe observed.

"I appreciate your insight." She picked up the rope, pulled herself onto Princess yet again and leaned close to the mare, rubbing her gently. "Cowboys think they know everything," she whispered. The horse whinnied in agreement.

Once again she prepared the rope, refining her loop and coil, stepping Princess in a bit tighter.

This time the rope sailed clear past the dummy.

"Momma, can we have lunch now?"

"Lunch? Yes." She smiled at Casey as she slid from the horse and retrieved the rope. "You go on in the house and wash up. I'll be in as soon as I rub down Princess."

"You know, that was pretty good considering you haven't held a rope in a dozen years," he said.

Rebecca coiled the rope and handed it to him. He dismounted and stood close without touching the offered rope.

"I mean it, Becca. That was a compliment. I don't hand them out on a regular basis."

She met his gaze. "Thank you."

"About that chocolate cake."

"What?" She blinked, confused.

"As I recall, you used to make blue-ribbon chocolate cakes. You said you're going to make one soon. I'm looking forward to a piece."

"My cake-baking skills are likely to be as rusty as my roping."

The corners of Joe's lips curved. "I'm guessing you haven't forgotten.

"I'll make a deal with you. Stop by tonight for a therapy session and I'll have chocolate cake ready."

"Therapy?"

"Take it or leave it."

"You drive a hard bargain."

She nodded, hiding a smile. "That I do."

"That's another kid's toy," Joe said.

"No. It's another therapy tool." Rebecca pushed the puzzle across the kitchen table to him, ignoring his irritation.

He glanced around. "Where's Casey?"

"She's getting ready for bed."

Joe released a breath. "Good, because I feel pretty silly."

"We use this one for manual dexterity. You aren't the first patient to utilize this tool. Simply pick up the shapes and place them in the right slot using your prosthetic hand. It's a repetition exercise to get you accustomed to using those muscles again."

"What muscles? I'm missing half my arm."

"You know what I mean. Your nerves still transmit the same signals as if the limb was there. All we're doing is reminding them again. The goal is to increase your control. The strength and speed of your response will increase as well, the more you practice."

"Whatever. Seems like a lot of work for chocolate cake."

"As you said, my cakes were blue ribbon winners." She glanced over at the counter, where the cake was cooling and waiting to be frosted.

"It better be for this," he muttered.

"You're doing an awful lot of complaining, considering you're whizzing right through all these exercises. I don't think you really appreciate all you have going for you."

"How so?"

"You have great range of motion. No medical problems. Your phantom limb pain is minimal. You have great skin integrity and muscle development. You're like a model patient."

"Except for my crummy attitude, right?"

"I didn't say that."

"No, I did."

Rebecca focused on documenting his activity in her tablet.

"Maybe I wouldn't have such a bad attitude if I wasn't responsible for all of this," he muttered.

"It was an accident. Accidents happen."

He met her eyes, his fingers poised in midair. "Do you know what happened?"

"I've not wanted to pry, though of course I've read your medical records."

"The fact is, I should have asked for help. I didn't. Simple as that." He shrugged. "I was repairing a tractor. The tractor fell on me."

"Oh, Joe." It was one thing to read a report, another to hear the words from his mouth. Pain cut through her, and she raised her hands to cover her mouth.

"I did it to myself. My mistake could have cost me the ranch. If Dan hadn't stepped in, I don't know what I would have done. He'd cashed out of his share years ago. Yet not only was he the first responder on the scene that day, but he was responsible for keeping the ranch running when I was in the hospital. I owe my brother plenty."

"I had no idea."

Joe nodded. "Family really is everything, Becca. Took me a while to fully appreciate that." He dropped the last piece in the slot. "Done."

"Actually, you have to do it twice more. I'll frost the cake while you finish."

"Maybe I should frost the cake," he said.

"Yes. Great idea. We'll let you bake a cake and frost it next time. That will really facilitate more bilateral limb usage."

"Oh, brother," he muttered.

She moved to the counter and pulled out a stainless-steel spatula and quickly frosted the sides and then the top of the cake, swirling the chocolate whipped frosting into little peaks. How long since she'd done this? Years. At least well before the trial.

"What do you want with your cake?"

"Milk would be good. Thanks."

She poured a glass of milk and brought it along with a hefty slice of cake to the table.

Joe snickered.

"Are you laughing at me?"

"I'm laughing at the frosting you planted on your face."

Rebecca turned to examine her reflection in the toaster and swiped at her face with a towel. She straightened. "All good?"

"Nice try. Almost as good as your roping."

"I got it all." She frowned. "Didn't I?"

He bit back a chuckle. "Not hardly."

"Fine," she huffed, tossing the towel to him.

Joe stood. "Hold still." He dabbed at her nose and then her cheek. "You've even got some on your ear. How do you frost a cake and get chocolate everywhere?"

"It takes a certain amount of skill, I admit. But I was rushing before you barked at me."

"I don't bark," Joe murmured. His face was intent as he leaned down to carefully wipe the frosting from her ear with gentle strokes of the terry-cloth towel. Rebecca peeked up at him from beneath her lashes. She shivered when she realized his lips hovered inches from hers.

Suddenly he sucked in a breath and stepped away.

"All done."

"Thanks," she said a little too brightly.

"Aren't you going to get Casey for cake?"

"Yes. Right away." Rebecca nodded and moved down the hallway to the pink bedroom. Right about now she could certainly use a buffer between herself and the handsome cowboy in her kitchen.

Chapter Eight

Joe glanced up at the Sunday afternoon sky as he rounded the corner of the barn. Becca was in the drive with her head beneath the hood of the battered Honda. He was feeling inordinately good today, and he supposed Casey and Becca had a lot to do with that

Go figure. He seemed unable to resist her and her little girl yesterday. It was a good day, even if he didn't get all the calls he needed to make completed. It didn't escape him that he and Becca could have had a child if things had worked out.

That was probably a road he'd best avoid going down. So he didn't. Instead, he shoved his hands in his pockets as he approached her, making as much noise as possible in an effort to keep from startling her. He inched closer, clearing his throat, yet Becca still didn't turn to acknowledge his presence. Finally he moved to the side of the car and put a gentle hand on her shoulder. That did it. She jumped, coming in immediate contact with the hood.

"Ouch." Her hand moved to her head. She pushed hair out of her face, neatly spreading grease across her cheek.

Earbuds.

That was why she hadn't heard him.

"I'm sorry." He mouthed the words.

"What?" Rebecca pulled the buds from her ears. "What did you say?"

"Sorry. I was actually trying not to startle you. You sure are jumpy."

"I guess I was concentrating." She rubbed her head one more time and pulled down the sleeves of her T-shirt.

"You okay? Maybe I should check your scalp, be sure you didn't do any serious damage."

"I'm fine." She waved him away with a hand. "By the way, I have a bone to pick with you."

"Fire away."

"You didn't tell me you have a rooster."

"Chickens, too. My mother's department." He rolled his eyes. "Woke you up?"

"Not me. I sleep through anything." Becca shook her head. "Casey woke me, determined to go find the rooster."

"So much for sleeping in, huh?"

"Exactly!" she said.

"Add that to your list of things that make ranch life so very special."

"Who takes care of the chickens while your mom is out of town?"

Joe grunted. "I don't do chickens. She hired a local high school student from the 4-H." He shoved his hands back in his pockets. "Other than the rooster, how's the house working out for you?"

"It's perfect, although that empty garden is a little depressing, and I wish I had time to put flowers in those pots."

"Pick up a few plants."

"Maybe. Though I'm not sure it would be worth the time and energy."

"It is if it matters to you."

"Yes. I suppose you're right." She looked him up and down. "You're awfully cheerful."

"Don't look so surprised."

"I am. You've been like a grizzly with a burr in his paw since I arrived."

"No, I haven't."

"Yes, you have."

He looked at the sky. "Maybe I am feeling good. Extended forecast says there might be a long window of sunshine coming up. I'm not holding my breath, but it could be enough time to get my hay harvested. That's enough to put anyone in a good mood." Joe paused. "Do you hear that?"

"Yes. It's coming from these." She lifted one of the earbuds that dangled around her neck.

"What is that you're listening to anyhow?"

She bit her lip and hesitated. "Italian opera."

"Why?"

"My father got me hooked on the stuff. He was a closet tenor. What a voice."

Joe shook his head. "A cowboy Pavarotti. That makes for an interesting visual."

She wiped her hands on a rag and offered a musing smile. "Yes, trust me, my father in a black Stetson singing Verdi's 'Celeste Aida' is a memory I will never forget."

"You're very fortunate to have such a relationship with your father."

"I always thought you and your father were close."

"We were. Most of the time. After all, we were Big Joe and Little Joe." He hesitated, choosing his words carefully as he met her gaze.

"When Dan left, my father was afraid I'd bolt, too. We're a fourth-generation ranching family, and I suppose he saw it all slipping away. I was a kid back then, but I was suffocating. So I joined the army."

"You eventually came back."

"Don't give me too much credit. I came back because he was dying."

"I'm sorry," she murmured.

"The thing is, I don't know if I would have done anything differently. That's what eats at me. I should feel more remorse. I don't. I know that I had to leave, so I could return." He took a deep breath. "Does that make any sense?"

"Yes. It does. More than you realize."

"It's like the life cycle of a ranch kid. You have to leave to appreciate what you left behind."

She stared at him. "I know this is a long time coming, but that's exactly how it was for me."

Joe stared at her. Suddenly his mood began a slow descent south. "What are you saying?" He asked the question that he wasn't sure he really wanted the answer to.

"I'm apologizing for how I treated you. Back then. I don't want to make excuses, but that's exactly how it was for me."

He narrowed his eyes and clamped his jaw.

"My father died. I certainly didn't have the legacy of a ranch like you did. In fact I felt as though I had nothing. No home anymore. No future here in Paradise." She released a sigh. "Nick offered me a chance to escape, a promising future with a man who cared for me. I took it."

Joe stepped back, creating even more distance between them.

"I'm not expecting your forgiveness. All I want to do is explain and apologize for how poorly I treated you."

"Duly noted."

An awkward silence stretched for moments. Becca turned to focus her attention inside the hood of the car.

"Having problems with the Honda?" Joe asked.

"It almost didn't make it out of the church parking lot this morning, which makes no sense. I had the alternator and the starter replaced in Alamosa."

"Battery?"

"Could be. My guess is it's as old as the car. Anyhow, I finished the oil change and was about to check."

"You change your own oil?"

"I do. Much less expensive that way."

"I guess you're a lot handier than I realized."

"Yes. I believe that was the point. Dad always thought he'd stay on Elliott Ranch as foreman until he retired, with me as his shotgun, but his ticker had other plans."

"I don't mean to keep bringing up sad memories."

"Not at all. I only have happy memories when it comes to my father." Becca stopped, her neck craning toward a sound overhead. "What is that?"

Joe shaded his eyes, turning his attention to the sky. A chocolate-brown bird with broad, rounded wings and a short, wide, red tail soared in a large circle, its wings barely moving. "Red-tailed hawk."

"Beautiful," she said. "Hey, and look at that sky. I'm guessing the threat of rain has passed."

"Yeah, I was plenty relieved to get up this morning to find that the storm had moved quickly to the north."

"I imagine so."

"I'm not going to bank on the rain holding off forever. We're at the end of June, which means precipitation is to be expected. In fact, there are a whole lot of folk in the valley praying for moisture."

"Anyone lined up to help with the hay?"

"I have calls to make today."

She cocked her head, listening. "Is that your phone?"

"No. I left mine in the house."

"Must be mine."

Becca patted her pockets before reaching into the car for the cell phone on the dash.

"Missed it." She pressed redial. "Mom?" Becca shook her head. "I had my earbuds in... Oh, my goodness. I better go get her." Seemingly annoyed, she shoved the phone into the back pocket of her jeans.

"What kind of mother am I?" she muttered. "My mom called twice. Apparently I also missed a call from Casey's other grandmother."

"Talk about being hard on yourself. That could have happened to anyone."

"Maybe, but I don't need to look any more incompetent than I already do in front of the Simpsons." Tools clanged as she haphazardly tossed them into the trunk.

"So what's going on?" Joe asked.

"Casey doesn't feel well. My mother is three hours away. I need to pick her up."

"Where is Casey?"

"The Simpson summer home in Four Forks. My mother dropped her off. They've got a huge graduation party going on. Virginia, that's Nick's mom, she was supposed to take Casey home, but she can't very well leave her guests."

"I can do Four Forks."

She bit her lip. "Oh, no. I couldn't ask you to drive all the way up there."

"The last thing you need is to drive to Four Forks and have your car quit."

"Your plan is to drive the farm truck?"

"No. I have a perfectly reputable new truck."

"That would be great. Thank you."

"Um, Becca?"

"Yes?"

"You've still got grease on your face. Maybe you should go clean up real quick."

"Yes. Yes. Of course." She glanced down at her clothes. "I better change, too. I don't want to stand out any more than necessary. I'll be fast."

"I'll get my truck and pull it around."

Becca started toward the cottage, then stopped. She turned back a few steps. "Joe?"

"Yeah?"

"I mean it. Thank you."

He nodded and watched her disappear into the house. She wouldn't be pleased to know that everything inside him was hollering to step up and protect her, shield her from a world that had treated her so badly. No, Becca Anshaw Simpson wouldn't be pleased at all. For now he was simply grateful that this one time she had allowed him to help. He wouldn't spend time wondering exactly why he felt the need to do it.

Rebecca quickly showered and slipped into slacks and a blouse. With a glance at the ugly, puckered vertical scar inside her right arm, she grabbed a long-sleeve white, cotton sweater before she met Joe outside.

The drive to Four Forks was silent. The scenery passed in a blur as her thoughts raced, anticipating a possible confrontation with Nick's family.

Joe slowed as they approached a sign indicating they were on the outskirts of Four Forks, and Rebecca began to reminisce about happier times navigating this same route.

The little town, twenty-five minutes north, had much less than half the population of Paradise. The standing joke was that Four Forks was a third the size of a postage stamp. The town thrived as a haven for crafters and artisans, bringing tourists in from all over the country.

"Which way?" he asked when they entered the center of the quaint town.

"Veer right when you hit the light. The road is a little hidden."

"Which light?"

She turned to him, brows raised. "There's only one intersection in Four Forks."

"I know. Lighten up. It was a joke. You're as tense as a cow heading to a branding party."

Rebecca relaxed for a moment before quickly leaning forward to point to the turnoff. "There it is. Do you see it?"

"Got it."

"The bad news is that it's a winding two-lane road up that hill."

Joe nodded, his gaze concentrated on the road.

"There's deer in the woods on either side of the road, and, of course, the shoulders are barely there, or nonexistent."

"The good news would be what?" Joe asked.

"The Simpsons own the only house up there, so there's very little traffic."

"I can imagine this is fun in the winter," Joe observed as he navigated cautiously.

"Winters are spent in Palm Springs."

"Sure they are. What was I thinking?"

After a quarter of a mile, the bumpy gravel road became a smoothly paved drive. Joe continued to steer the truck past a long row of conifers and a succession of cars parked bumper-to-bumper. As they drove around a curve, a home came into view, set back behind a huge wrought-iron security gate that was spread across the massive drive.

Camelot. That was what she used to call the sprawling, ranch-style mansion with the impressive columns. As Nick Simpson's wife, she used to be among the royal family that claimed seasonal residency here.

Joe gave a low whistle. "So this is how the other half lives."

"Gallagher Ranch isn't exactly low-rent. Why, you have three houses on that land."

He nodded. "Yeah, and they could all fit inside this one. Who did you say calls this home?"

"My former mother-in law, Virginia Simpson."

"Her husband?"

"Nicholas Sr. died when the children were young."

Joe didn't ask, and she wasn't going to divulge that Nick's father had shared the family disease. Alcoholism.

"How do we get through the gate?"

"They have a guard on duty during events. He'll have my name." Rebecca glanced around. "You can park wherever there's an open spot. I can walk from here."

Joe eased the car along the side and unbuckled his seat belt.

"Um, Joe, it's best if you stay in the truck," she stated. "I may run into Judge Brown, and he certainly won't make it easy."

"I was going to stay in the truck until you said that."

She leaned back against the seat. "I'm giving you sound advice, and you're ignoring me."

He winked, offering an exaggerated squaring of his shoulders. "I think maybe I can handle myself, and I have no intention of letting you into the corral with a bull all by yourself."

"Fine. Fine. But don't say anything. Your presence

alone will be intimidating." She unbuckled her seat belt. "This is Nick's sister's party. College graduation. My plan is to get in and out without a family argument."

"Sounds like an excellent idea to me." He narrowed his eyes in thought. "We go up to the house to get Casey. My job is to look intimidating without opening my mouth. Do I have that straight?"

She released a breath. "That wasn't quite what I said."

"No?" Joe pushed his ball cap to the back of his head.

"No. We'll pass that security guard together. Then you can stand a discreet distance back in case I need help with Casey."

He opened the door of the truck. "That's what I said."

Rebecca took a last look at her appearance in the visor mirror before flipping it back into place. By the time she had opened her door, Joe was there to offer her a hand down to the grassy ground on her side of the vehicle. She met his gaze.

"Thank you," she breathed.

"You know, I could go up there and get Casey for you," he said. "Save you all this anxiety."

She stepped down, gathering her confidence as she straightened the collar of her blouse. "No. I have to do this. I'm sure I'm making more out of this situation than it deserves—however, I haven't talked to any of Nick's family since court."

Two months ago, she mused. Two months since she'd been found innocent. She'd moved the mountain with God's help then, and she would do it again if necessary. It wasn't Joe Gallagher's job to fight her battles for her.

They walked through the gate with a wordless nod from the guard, whose eyes voiced disapproval in one sweeping glance.

"Talkative guy." Joe shaded his eyes and glanced up

at the house. "Only five more miles to the front door," he muttered.

In the distance Rebecca could hear music. No doubt a live band or a small orchestra. The Simpsons didn't do anything on a small scale. The closer she got to the house, the louder the buzz of voices and partying from behind the house became.

Rebecca remembered being part of the festivities once. She'd had her wedding reception here. Tents had been set up on the endless lush lawn behind the house. Flowers had been flown in. Expensive catering ordered. They'd pulled out all the stops for Judge Brown's grandson.

Her engagement ring alone had been embarrassingly huge. She'd worn a dress of flowing lace and a simple tiara with a net veil that day, along with Nick's promise of a future together.

Tall, fair and utterly charming, Nick Simpson had provided the complete package. He'd served up every girl's dream come true on a glass platter.

Except that dream had ultimately turned into a nightmare that crashed into a million cutting pieces, and her prince became someone she barely recognized.

As they approached the house, Rebecca wrapped her arms around herself and shivered. She quickened her pace, leaving Joe behind to wait near the large water fountain in the center of the drive as she moved up the walk and up the steps to the front door.

Moments after she rang the bell, the massive oak door opened and she was face-to-face with Judge Nicholas Brown.

Rebecca swallowed hard. When her heart began to beat a furious tempo, she stepped back several paces.

"You." The word was fairly spat in her direction as his

probing black eyes seared her with a nameless though oh-so-familiar accusation.

Yet something was different about the judge. Rebecca met the piercing gaze. Refusing to look away, she assessed the older man. She hadn't seen Nick's grandfather since their day in court. At that time, she'd barely had the courage to look him in the eye.

He'd changed. Not only was his color off, the skin sallow, but he seemed smaller than she remembered a mere few months ago. Suddenly realization hit her. Rebecca had lost Nick slowly, painfully over several years. By the time she'd buried her husband, he was a stranger. But Judge Brown had lost his grandson in one tragic split-second accident. She should have been praying for this poor man.

"Sir, I'm here to pick up my daughter."

Judge Brown looked past her to where Joe stood a few feet away, watching.

"I see you brought your bodyguard with you."

Rebecca turned in time to see Joe's jaw clench. She gave a quick shake of her head to keep him from jumping to her defense.

A moment later, Virginia appeared. A grimace of embarrassment crossed her face when she glanced from her father to Rebecca. She placed a gentle hand on her father's shoulder.

"Judge, why don't you go back to the party? Jana was asking about you."

Rebecca released the breath she'd been holding, her attention fixed on the judge as he disappeared into the house.

"Won't you come in?" Virginia offered. "I'm sure Jana would love to see you."

"I'm fine here. Thank you. Casey?"

"I think she overindulged. She's been resting. My assistant has gone to get her."

Virginia clasped her palms together. She glanced down the drive at Joe, her eyes registering confusion before her gaze returned to Rebecca.

"Please excuse my father," Virginia said. The words were soft and apologetic.

"I don't blame you for his actions, Virginia."

"Maybe you should. He's my father and I… Well, it wasn't until that last day in court that I realized what my inability to stand up to him had ultimately done to Nick—" she hesitated "—as well as to you and Casey, and your family."

"It's not easy. I understand."

"No. You shouldn't understand." Virginia waved a hand in a gesture of frustration. "I knew the accident wasn't your fault. I should have stopped him. I should have asked for your forgiveness long before today, too."

Rebecca reached out and laid a hand on Virginia's arm. "I turned this over to God a long, long time ago. Maybe you should, as well."

"Yes. Yes. You're right," Virginia whispered. Her blue eyes were filled with pain and unshed tears. She turned as a young woman approached with Casey by her side.

Rebecca's heart clutched. The party dress Casey wore was rumpled, as though she'd been sleeping. "Oh, baby, are you okay?"

Her daughter nodded all the while rubbing her stomach with a hand. "My tummy hurts."

Rebecca gently pushed Casey's bangs aside and laid her hand on her daughter's forehead. The damp skin burned with heat. There was more than a stomachache going on here.

"Let's go home," she said, with a nod of thanks to Virginia.

As they headed down the drive, Joe walked up to meet them.

"Look, Joe's here," Casey murmured, a small smile brightening her wan features.

"Yes. Joe's here," Rebecca said.

Joe met Rebecca's gaze. "You handled that nicely."

"Thank you," she returned.

He knelt in front of her little girl. "How about if I carry you to the truck?"

"Yes. Please," Casey said.

Joe walked down the long drive past the guard to the truck with Casey cradled in his arms.

Rebecca knew it was a memory she wouldn't soon forget. "Oh, dear Lord," she whispered. "Thank you for a friend like Joe Gallagher."

Chapter Nine

"Gentlemen. We need to talk." Joe stood in the doorway and crossed his arms.

Rod and Julian both froze and slowly turned to look at him. They stood at attention beside the long metal table set up in the equipment garage. Laptops, cameras and video equipment littered the makeshift work space where they reviewed each day's footage.

Neither man uttered a word in response to his announcement.

"Becca suggested I let you film moving the cows to the fresh pasture."

Rod let out a breath. "I thought we were in trouble again."

Julian paled. "How are we going to do that?" He fiddled with his glasses.

"You two can ride the farm truck and film."

Becca walked into the garage, excitement in her eyes at his words. "You're going to let me help herd?"

"What are you doing here? What about Casey?"

"I took her to the doctor. Whatever she had has disappeared. My mother took her to Pueblo, to the zoo."

"Are you sure you don't want to take the day off? You could go with them."

"I've already missed the entire morning."

"You don't punch a clock. Besides, I moved most of the herd already."

"You did?"

Joe nodded. "There's still a slight chance of rain until the end of the week. I had to. I've got about fifty or so stragglers left, if that makes you feel better. The plan is to gently encourage them back to the pasture. I'll ride Blackie and pull up the rear with the dogs." He met Becca's gaze. "Would you be willing to ride outside the herd?"

"Sure," she said.

"The dogs and I will be zigzagging back and forth." He looked pointedly at Rod and Julian. "Keep the truck away from the cows."

"What about me?" Abi asked as she joined them.

"You can come along, as long as you promise not to put any videos on YouTube," Joe said.

"That hardly seems fair," she murmured with feigned indignation.

Joe only chuckled as they all exited the garage. He slowed his pace to match Becca's stride as they crossed the yard to the horses together.

"Sorry I couldn't wait for you. Eighty percent chance of precipitation predicted for later this afternoon. I'm watching for a four-day stretch of sunshine before I hit full harvest mode. We may have it toward the end of the week."

"Have you had any confirmations from your contacts?"

"Funny thing about that," Joe said. "Suddenly everyone is previously committed."

Rebecca gasped. *"Judge Brown."*

"Not necessarily, but, yeah, that was my initial thought, as well."

"It's because of me. I feel terrible about this, Joe. What are you going to do?"

"We'll find a way. Always do."

They saddled up the horses and headed out toward the pasture.

Joe whistled for the dogs and picked up his pace, trotting Blackie in the other direction. "There they are," he called out. Straight ahead the last of the herd had gathered near the water trough, with a few stragglers near the creek.

"The dogs and I will rustle along those near the creek, then I'll head to the front to turn them around. You're okay working the outside?"

"Of course," she answered. "I've got things covered. Don't worry."

"But I do worry," Joe muttered. "I worry plenty."

"Where's the truck?" Becca called to Joe.

"Here it comes." He pointed a gloved hand behind them. The truck slowly approached with Rod seated in the flatbed with his camera as Julian drove and Abi rode shotgun.

Becca called out to Rod and Julian. "Joe is going to turn the cows and start the forward movement. Stay back from the herd. I'll be moving toward them once he gets things turned around."

"Why would you move toward them?" Rod asked.

"Cattle will move in the opposite direction of a perceived threat or predator." She turned in the saddle. "Julian, stay back so we don't spook them or the horses. And don't get out of the truck. You'll be crushed if you're in the wrong place and they get agitated."

"Crushed? There's a chance of getting crushed? I'm not too sure this is in my job description," Julian returned.

"Follow Becca's instructions and you'll be fine," Joe said. We just don't want you to find yourself between a cow and her calf."

"No worries. We're all staying in the truck," Rod said. "Those cows look pretty big to me."

"They may be big, but they aren't all that smart. Try to remember that cowboys have been doing this for a very long time."

"You'd have thought they'd come up with a better plan than this after two or three hundred years," Rod observed.

Joe chuckled at the comment as he and the dogs pushed past the cows to the front. Gil and Wishbone nipped at the heels of the animals, encouraging them along and turning them around. Joe gave a nod of satisfaction. Finally something was going right.

As the first of the herd plodded along, moving along the trail to the new pasture, Julian called out from the truck. *"Rawhide."* His face was bright with excitement.

Rod offered a hearty thumbs-up to Joe as he filmed.

This was good. They'd get their footage, and he'd get his herd moved.

Becca continued to encourage the herd along, riding Princess on the outside, right where they could see her and out of the cattle's blind spot. "Come on," she encouraged the cows "You've done this before. Let's move nice and steady. We'll be done real quick."

"You talking to yourself?" Joe hollered.

"Yes. I am. You talk to the dogs."

"That's true," he returned with a smile of satisfaction. Moments later, Julian hollered from the truck window and waved his arms. His panicked voice rang out. "Joe, behind you. Those cows are headed off in the wrong direction. What should I do?"

"Easy, there Julian," Joe called back. "We don't worry about stragglers. Relax, buddy. The dogs and I will catch them later."

The blare of the truck's horn blasted into the air.

"No," Joe yelled. "Don't use the horn. You'll spook the…"

Becca's horse was closest to the truck. At the sound Princess reared with panic, nostrils flaring. Eyes wild, the mare snorted and galloped in a circle with Becca struggling desperately to soothe the animal and rein her in. Princess circled one more time before taking off with Becca clinging to the reins.

"Get the truck away from the herd," Joe called to Julian, his full attention on Becca.

The rumble of hooves on the ground drowned his voice as the remaining cows began to stampede. He wasn't concerned about the small herd. It was Becca who had his full attention. His heart thundered as he raced Blackie after them.

"No. No. No," he whispered. "Not Becca. Not now."

Princess and Becca continued their wild ride. When the horse and rider approached a thicket of trees, the mare suddenly stopped, the action tossing Becca into the air as though she were weightless. She landed against a fallen tree branch.

Joe slid off his horse and raced to where she lay on her side, sprawled on the ground still muddy from last week's rain. He skidded to a stop in the mud, kneeling next to her. Her hat and phone were scattered on the ground, and her body was twisted awkwardly. He was terrified to move her.

He tore off his gloves using his teeth and felt her neck for a pulse. "Oh, Lord," he murmured. "Please, please don't let her die on me."

"I am not dead."

"Becca?" Joe blinked.

When her lashes fluttered, relief pounded through him.

She moaned and rolled to her back. "Ouch."

"What hurts?" he asked.

"What doesn't?"

With a gentle motion, he elevated her shoulder to release the limb that was still twisted behind her.

"Much better. Thank you." She tried to sit up and groaned, easing back down. "Oh, man, I'm dizzy. This is definitely not how I planned to spend my day."

"Stay still," Joe said. He carefully patted her down from head to foot. The back of her head boasted a lump, though the skin remained intact.

"Can you move your legs?"

Eyes closed, she wiggled her boots.

"Thank you, God," Joe said aloud.

"I see you two are talking again," Becca murmured.

"This isn't funny," he ground out. For once, he was grateful for the rain. With the exception of a few jagged rocks from the gravel and dirt road, the ground was cushioned with soft grass and thick mud where she'd landed.

He checked her extremities. All intact except her right arm. Red seeped through a long-sleeve shirt. Joe swallowed hard, fear rising within him. He grasped the fabric with both hands until the cotton tore, allowing him to push the material out of the way enough to evaluate the injury.

A gash at least six inches long bled steadily, but didn't appear to have severed any major blood vessels. Beside the cut, a long, disfiguring scar trailed the inside of Becca's arm. She'd injured herself before?

"Here." A cotton gauze pad was thrust at him.

Joe looked up. Abi stood over them. "Where'd you get this?"

"First-aid kit in the truck."

"Thanks." He applied the pad to Becca's arm and then pulled a cotton handkerchief from his pocket, securing the gauze in place.

"Will she be all right?" Abi asked on a near sob.

"There doesn't seem to be anything broken. I'm not a doctor, and that was some fall she took. No doubt she has a concussion."

"It's not nice to talk about me like I'm not here," Becca whispered, her eyes still closed.

"Oh, Rebecca," Abi said, kneeling down. "That was quite a scare."

Becca reached out a hand, and Abi took it.

"I'm going to be fine," Becca said.

"I'm counting on it," Abi returned.

"Is Rod okay?" Joe asked. "Did Julian get the truck out of the way?"

"Rod's fine. Shaken up, but fine. He nearly fell out of the flatbed once Julian hit the gas pedal."

"And Julian?"

"Julian is a mess, blubbering that he killed Rebecca."

"Oh, brother."

Abi released Becca's hand and stood. "Yeah, tell me about it. What do you want me to do, Joe?"

"Call 9-1-1. Tell them Gallagher Ranch. North access road. Then park the truck there so you can direct them. The north access is the gate Rod stumbled on the first day. Think you can find it?"

"I've got it."

"Thanks, Abi. Oh, and get Rod and Julian back to the house, as well."

"No problem."

An agitated whinny indicated that Princess had returned. Joe stood and pulled the dragging reins from the mud, tying the leather to a tree. "Easy, girl. Easy. It's all over now." He murmured more soothing words as he stroked the mare.

A phone rang and Joe scrambled around on the ground until he found the device. Mud covered the screen. He could let it go to voice mail, but what if it was important? What if it was her mother? Becca would want him to take the call if it was about something important.

"My phone?" she murmured.

"I found it, Becca." He held it to his ear. "Hello?"

"You need to get out of Paradise. You aren't wanted here."

"Who is this?" Joe demanded.

The call disconnected.

There was no doubt in his mind that the voice on the other end of the unidentified call was Judge Brown. He stared at the phone. Did that call mean that the Judge had threatened Becca before? He was going to find out, and right away.

In the distance, the wailing siren of the Paradise Valley ambulance echoed. Moments later, another siren sounded as well, indicating that someone from the sheriff's department was also on his way.

"Becca, open your eyes."

"No need to yell. I'm right here," she said.

"Can you see me?"

She opened her eyes and blinked. "Yes. It hurts to look, but I can see you very clearly." Her eyes closed again. "Stop frowning."

"I called an ambulance, Becca."

"No. I can't afford an ambulance. I'm perfectly capable of getting up."

He put a gentle, yet firm hand on her shoulder when she attempted to rise to a seated position. "Don't move."

"Yes, sir."

"We're not taking any chances. That was quite a fall."

She nodded slowly, her eyes wide open now.

Joe looked deep into her brown eyes. Today they were the color of the pecans harvested on the ranch in the autumn. His hands stopped shaking long enough for him to gently push the hair away from her face, and wipe a dab of mud from her chin. A bruise was starting to color her forehead.

"I'm a real mess, huh?"

"You look beautiful," Joe whispered as he untangled a mass of her dark hair.

He froze, and his breath hitched. The words "and I love you," had nearly slipped from his lips.

In that moment, he realized that he had never stopped loving Rebecca Anshaw. Twelve long years and he loved her as much as when he was a kid.

Joe sighed and shook his head.

"What's wrong?" Becca murmured.

"Nothing at all."

Nothing at all, except now he had one more thing to keep him awake at night.

"Why do I need an IV?" Rebecca asked the nurse.

"That cowboy who brought you in indicated you lost a lot of blood, so the doctor wanted to be safe. Besides, a little normal saline makes everything better, don't you think?"

"I'll take your word for it." Rebecca sat quietly on the gurney as the fluid dripped into the tubing.

"Don't you want to lie down?" the nurse asked.

"No. I feel fine. My vision is back to normal. When can I go home?"

"Your arm isn't sutured yet, but I imagine Dr. Rogers will release you once she has the X-ray and CT scan results."

"Dr. Rogers? What happened to the doctor who examined me when I came in? The one who did that neuro exam."

"Oh, you know. Shift change. Dr. Rogers is taking over. She says she's a friend of yours."

"Dr. Rogers?"

"Sara Elliott Rogers."

"Oh, Sara Elliott." Rebecca smiled. "Yes. We practically grew up together on her father's ranch."

"Well, then. That's good news. She'll be here in a moment."

On cue, the door opened and her old friend walked in. Sara Elliott Rogers looked exactly the same as Rebecca remembered. Petite with a smattering of freckles on her face, and black hair pulled back into a French braid.

"Marta, thanks for cleaning up that wound. I'll finish up." She turned to Rebecca. "This is a terrible way to catch up with an old friend."

"Sara!"

"Easy. Stay on that gurney." Sara moved over to offer her a hearty hug. "I've missed you, cowgirl." She moved back to assess Rebecca and frowned. "That's going to be some bruise in the middle of your forehead. Sort of like old times, right? We certainly got a lot of scrapes and shiners on the ranch, didn't we?"

"Yes. We did. What's this I hear about you having twins? Is that right?" Rebecca asked.

"Yes. They're almost two now. I'm going a little crazy trying to keep up with them. I've cut back to working part-time here and at the Paradise Clinic."

"We'll have to plan to get together. I'd love to see them."

"Absolutely." Sara donned a pair of gloves. "So the nurse cleaned up your wound. All we have to do is stitch you up." She turned to assess the suture kit laid out and ready. "Why don't you lay back and get comfortable."

Rebecca rested against the small gurney pillow.

"Any dizziness when you reclined?"

"No, that seems to have gone away."

"Good. The CT appears normal. However, you'll want to restrict your activity for the next week. No horseback riding until you're cleared. We'll give you a checklist of symptoms that might indicate you need to come back in to the emergency room or the clinic immediately."

"No horseback riding?"

"No. I know that seems restrictive, but we certainly don't want another concussion before this one heals. We'll reevaluate when you come in for a follow-up in the clinic."

Rebecca was silent as Sara's gentle fingers probed the length of the wound.

"I think we're looking at about twelve stitches. First you're going to feel a little needle prick as I administer the anesthetic.

"Doing okay?" Sara asked a moment later.

"I'm good."

"This is going to be to the left of this scar you already have."

Rebecca tensed as Sara inspected the ugly vertical line.

"Who did that last suture job?"

"It was a teaching hospital in Denver. I believe the physician was a student."

"Oh, goodness, let's hope he didn't decide to go into surgery. You might want to consider having a plastic surgeon evaluate the other incision line for revision. We can do much better that that."

"It's no big deal," Rebecca murmured. She was silent as Sara worked, praying against all odds that she wouldn't mention the ugly mark on her arm again.

"Tying off the sutures now. I promise you this one will be pretty. I crochet in my spare time."

Rebecca couldn't resist a smile.

"All done. Let me help you sit up." Sara removed her gloves and assisted her to a sitting position.

"Looks great," Rebecca said, as she inspected the thin, flat line of sutures.

"Thank you. Keep it clean and dry. You can cover it loosely to protect the area. I'll give you some ointment and extra gauze pads and tape. Apply the ointment to the area once a day, sparingly. Then, as I said, I'll see you in a week in the clinic for follow-up."

"Okay," Rebecca said quietly.

Sara washed and dried her hands at the sink. She grabbed the clipboard chart. "I want to talk to you about the X-ray results."

"My X-rays?"

"You have no new fractures."

"That's good, right?"

Sara met her gaze. "Rebecca, your X-ray shows indications that the right arm has been broken several times. In at least one of those events, the bone was not properly set."

Rebecca began to tremble "Yes. A few accidents."

"The scar on your arm?"

Rebecca turned her head away and closed her eyes tightly, waiting for what she knew would come next.

"I'm required by law to report suspected cases of abuse."

"Why?" she whispered. "Nick is dead."

Sara inhaled sharply and put her hand on Rebecca's shoulder. "Oh, honey. I'm so sorry."

Shame washed over Becca as she stared at the pattern on the hospital gown. "Please, please, don't tell anyone."

"There's no need for me to. The threat is gone. There are laws that protect your health-care privacy. However, I am going to give you a card. I want you to get counseling."

"I've had counseling. With God's help I'm healing."

"Take the card. You never know. If there's anything I can do . ."

"Thank you, Sara."

Rebecca hid her face as Sara finished writing on the chart.

"Rebecca, I am looking forward to getting together. Will I see you at the Fourth of July barbecue?"

"I guess I forgot about that."

"You have been gone awhile. No one forgets about my father's barbecue. I'll look for you."

She nodded, waiting for shame to engulf her again as the door quietly closed behind Sara.

Yet this time words of scripture bubbled up from inside. *Do not remember the former things, nor consider the things of old.*

"Oh, Lord," she prayed. "I'm ready."

Joe paced the emergency department waiting room of Paradise Valley Hospital. He glanced one more time at his watch.

Sure the place was busy, but it had been an hour since the last update from the nurse. He'd called Joan Anshaw, and she was on her way home. He'd also stepped outside and had a long conversation with God. Basically he'd negotiated what he considered a real good deal. If He'd take care of Becca, Joe would plant himself in church on Sundays.

Desperate times predicated he stoop lower than usual. And he was definitely desperate.

Joe ran a hand over his face. When he raised his head, he noticed a door open in the examination area. Hopeful, he stepped closer.

Finally a nurse appeared. When she turned around, he could see that Becca was the patient in the wheelchair she was pushing.

Becca's gaze met his, and she offered him a small pitiful smile. Her hair was a tangled mess, and her clothes were covered with mud. The bruise on her forehead was now a purple beacon. Joe released his breath in a whoosh and shook his head, saying a silent prayer of thanks.

It only took a minute to pull his truck around.

"Maybe I should lift you," he said as he opened the passenger door.

"No. I can get in by myself."

"I won't bite," Joe murmured.

"Says who?"

"I know lots of people who will vouch…" He paused. "Okay, maybe only one or two." Joe smiled as he carefully closed the door behind her before jogging to the driver side.

"I can't believe they released you," he said, as he backed out of the drop-off zone.

"Joe, I'm fine. They wouldn't have discharged me if I wasn't ready to go home."

"Okay, but you're going to rest."

"Now you sound like my mother," she said as she fastened her seat belt.

"I happen to recall that your mom is a pretty terrific person, so you can try to insult me all you want. You're still going to rest."

Becca began to laugh. "That wasn't an insult. Simply a commentary. And yes, my mom is still amazing."

"Finally we agree on something." He paused. "How many stitches?"

"Twelve."

"Twelve! You won't be doing ranch work anytime soon," he growled.

"Someone a little grumpy?"

"Maybe so. I tend to get grumpy when I'm irritated."

"Why are you irritated?"

He glanced at her and frowned, shaking his head. *Because my heart was ripped out of my chest when you flew off that horse. That's why.*

They were silent as his truck smoothly headed toward Gallagher Ranch.

"Are you cold?" he finally asked, his voice gruff.

"Maybe a little."

"I brought your sweater. Abi's idea," he said. "Don't want you to think I'm going all thoughtful on you." He reached in the backseat and handed it to her.

"No, of course not," she murmured.

"I'll turn on the heat, too."

"Thank you, Joe." She awkwardly pulled the sweater over her shoulders. "Have you heard from my mom? Is Casey all right? They aren't worried, are they?"

"Joan will meet us at the ranch. I've been calling her with updates. Told her you landed on your head. She agreed with me that fortunately, since you're extremely hardheaded, there's no doubt you're going to be fine."

Becca chuckled and turned to him. "Thank you, again."

"My pleasure. I do it for all my hardheaded friends."

"Do you have many hardheaded friends?"

"You'd be surprised." He shot her a wink, feeling some of the anger subside. "Oh, and I have Julian tied up in the barn until I get back to the ranch, as a precautionary measure.

"Tell me you're kidding."

"I'll let you decide."

"Do you happen to know where my phone is?"

"Yeah, I've got it in a plastic bag in the backseat. The thing is covered with mud."

"Does it still work?"

"Oh, yeah." Joe cleared his throat. "Ah, Becca?"

"Yes?"

"What happened to your arm?"

"You know what happened to my arm."

"I'm talking about the other scar."

Becca tugged the sweater even closer. "That was a long time ago."

"I didn't ask you when it happened," he said slowly and softly. "I asked you what happened."

"Joe, do we have to discuss this now?"

He gripped the steering wheel tightly, struggling to hold back his anger. "Nick did it, didn't he?"

"It was an accident." The words were flat. Rote. Like she'd said them a dozen times before.

"What kind of accident gives you a scar like that, I wonder?"

"Glass. Shards of glass. I tripped and landed on a glass-topped table."

She didn't even stumble over the explanation. That more than anything caused a cold rage to start inside him.

Joe hit the brakes, automatically stretching out his prosthetic arm to keep Becca from pitching forward. Then he carefully eased the truck off the road.

His pent-up frustration was back, and it echoed in the truck, as he released a loud groan of pain. "Am I the only one who's figured out that your husband was hurting you?"

"No. No. No." The words were barely a whisper. A slow tear wound its way over her cheek and landed on her shirt collar.

It was Joe's undoing. He unbuckled his seat belt and wrapped his arms around her, resting her head against his chest.

The only sound was of the occasional vehicle passing by on the road.

"Casey must never know," Becca whispered against his chest.

"Why haven't you told Nick's grandfather? Surely that would get him off your case."

She eased back in her seat and fiddled with the buttons on her sweater. "Judge Brown would never believe me."

"He still should be told the truth."

"No, Joe."

"If you don't, then I will."

"Why? What good can possibly come of breaking an old man's heart?"

"That old man needs to stop harassing you. That's why. I accidently picked up a call he made to you on your phone. Becca, he's called you at least a dozen times. That's plain crazy. He's making your life miserable, and you don't deserve this."

"Please. Please. Promise me you won't tell him."

He shook his head. "I can't make that kind of promise. What kind of friend would I be if I agreed to that?"

"Joe, promise me you will not tell the judge."

He slammed a hand on the steering wheel, and she jumped.

"Look what he's done to you. You're jumpy as all getout these days. You never used to be like this."

"I've done it to myself. Besides, I'm not the same 'me' that you remember so well. That 'me' disappeared a long time ago."

"*A long time ago.* Yeah, I remember saying the same thing the day you showed up on the ranch. But you know what, Becca? I'm starting to realize that it's not so long ago after all. And really, deep down inside, we haven't changed as much as we'd like to believe."

She stared at him, her brown eyes round, her jaw set. "Joe?" she pleaded.

"All I can say is that I'm not too happy to find out you think you need to have all these secrets. You and I will revisit this conversation again. After you're feeling better and those greenhorns are on their way back to wherever it is they came from."

He started the truck and checked over his shoulder for oncoming vehicles. "Tonight, that's pretty much all I'm willing to guarantee."

Chapter Ten

Joe strode into Sheriff Sam Lawson's office, turned on the fan and checked to be sure the door was shut tight.

"Whoa. What's going on?" Sam asked.

"Becca is being harassed by Judge Brown."

"Are you sure?"

"I have proof," Joe returned.

"The man has to be seventy-five, eighty years old. Do you really think he's got the energy to do that?"

Joe shook his head and sank into a chair. "Yeah, I do. I'd probably be on the mark if I were to say revenge is the fuel that's keeping that man alive."

Sam's grimaced. "He's probably found six dozen Bible verses to support his actions. The thing about bitterness is that it's a disease that kills you by eating you from the inside out."

"You sound familiar with it."

"Saw it firsthand with my stepfather." He gave a shake of his head. "What a waste of a life."

"I'm sorry, Sam. I didn't realize."

The other man shrugged. "I don't talk about him much because I'm a little scared that after living with the guy for seventeen years, I might have the propensity to be like him."

"Not you, Sam. Never."

"I don't know.

"Trouble with this situation is that Judge Brown isn't about to give up until he breaks Becca."

"That's sad because his focus is on revenge, which means the other people in his life are ignored."

"No doubt." Joe took off his Stetson, ran his fingers along the crown crease and put it back on. "I've got another issue needling at me, as well. I have reason to believe Nick Simpson was physically abusing his wife."

"Joe, that's a pretty strong accusation." Sam took a deep breath. "Not one that you can get much traction out of, either, since the man is dead."

"I know. It galls me that I know I'm right and Becca refuses to tell anyone. I'm certain that one look at her medical records would show a pattern of abuse. Typically they're in and out of a variety of emergency rooms and urgent-care facilities. Women in that situation don't like to seek treatment at the same place twice."

"How'd you get so knowledgeable on the topic?"

"I called a counselor friend today. Same person I spoke with when I lost my arm."

"I didn't realize you went to therapy."

"Yeah, my doctor basically delivered an ultimatum."

"Smart doc, if he realizes that's the only way to get you to do anything."

"Thanks for the vote of confidence."

Sam narrowed his eyes, and his mouth formed a grim line.

"What are you thinking?" Joe asked his friend.

"I hate to even go down this road, but ninety to nothing this would explain the accident that killed Nick Simpson."

"You mean the abuse?"

Sam nodded. "Something just isn't right about how that all went down."

"Yeah, I've been thinking about that, too. Every time I do, it makes me so angry I can barely see straight. I have to do something." He met Sam's gaze. "What would you do about Judge Brown if you were in my position?"

"There's nothing we can do inside the law, unless Rebecca is willing to file a complaint."

"Which she won't do." Joe stood and paced across the office. "Isn't what he's doing considered criminal mischief or something?"

"No, that would be if he actually did damage."

"He's doing damage all right."

"Physical damage, I mean. Keying a car. Graffiti. Tire slashing. That generally falls under criminal mischief. While I would tend to agree with you, Joe, my hands are tied."

"Then I'm between a rock and a hard place." He clenched his left hand. "There has to be a way around this."

"Go talk to him."

"She won't let me. Arm wrestled me with tears."

"That'll do it every time."

Joe nodded. "She's not willing to open the door to her past again. Trouble is, it's not going to go away on its own."

"Could you go talk to the daughter? Nick's mother. Maybe talk around the topic until it's clear she understands your point. That wouldn't be breaking your promise, would it?"

"That might work. I'm going to have to pray on it.

There's a lot of gray around this whole mess. Either way, I owe you one. Thanks for letting me talk this through."

"Naw, I owe you one. I should have gotten those city people lost instead of taking them to your ranch. What was I thinking? They'd still be driving around in circles if I wasn't so hospitable. I've got to stop that. Being nice is my downfall."

Joe raised a brow as he slid back down into the chair. "What about that strawberry-blond writer who's crushing on you?"

"Well, I might make an exception for Miss Warren." When Sam smiled, a glint of amusement shone in his eyes.

"I suspected as much. What do you think about Abi?"

"What I think is that I've got enough going on in my life. I don't need a city girl. To that end, I'm doing my best to stay out of her way. The woman is smart, beautiful, yields a killer smile and, to make it worse, she's nice. That's a dangerously potent combination."

"Yeah, I heard you've been doing a lot of fishing lately."

Sam leaned forward in his chair and folded his hands on his desk. "I call that self-preservation. Fishing preserves my way of life. Besides, I like being single."

"Do you?"

"Sure I do," Sam said. "Don't you?"

"I don't know anymore. Maybe my brother, Dan, has it right. Either way, sure is a lot of that stuff going around lately. You notice?"

"You mean love and marriage?" Sam laughed. "There ought to be a vaccination for what causes that. Don't you think?"

"Too late for most of the men in town. Look at Jake

MacLaughlin. Bitsy is not only his stepmother, but her machinations got him and his wife together."

"Bitsy didn't have to do much. That man fell pretty hard."

"Doesn't look too unhappy about it, either," Joe observed.

"There's only a few of us left. You, me, Deke Andrews, Duffy McKenna. We're a dying breed."

"Ever occur to you that maybe we're just dinosaurs, Sam?"

"No. I like my life the way it is. Content. That's what I am."

"Content my boots! If you're content, it's because the sorry life you have is less frightening than taking a chance on you-know-what."

Sam cocked his head and nodded. "I won't rule out the possibility that you're right. Then again, I'll deny it if you tell anyone we even had this conversation." He pointed to the door. "And don't even let Bitsy get wind of it."

All Joe could do was laugh.

Joe pulled up the ten-day forecast on his laptop and released the breath he was holding. Finally things were looking good. Sunshine promised for the Fourth of July holiday and into all of next week.

"Thank You, Lord. If I don't say it enough times, thank You."

The hay would dry out, and then he'd be able to move the windrower through. A few days of drying, raking and he'd be able to bale.

Joe pulled up the number of Shady Malone, a friend who had helped him and Dan in the past. Shady and a couple of his friends did extra work on the local ranches in the Four Corners area.

"Shady, it's Joe Gallagher."

"Joe! How's it going?"

"Fine. Fine. I haven't heard back from you. Did you get my messages? Can I count on you this year? I'm looking at next week. The weather looks like it's finally going to cooperate."

"I'd like to help you Joe, 'cept me and the boys have contracted elsewhere."

"Really? You usually manage to juggle a couple of jobs at once, what with the time between cutting and baling."

The line was silent. "Joe, I like you. Gallagher Ranch has treated me well over the years. I'm not going to play games. The honest truth is that I'm being paid not to help you. Good money, too. Real good money."

Joe sat up in his chair, not believing what he was hearing. "Whoa. Whoa. You're kidding, right?"

"I wish I was. If I don't play ball, I'm going to be blackballed in the valley."

"Judge Brown?"

"Don't know about that. I was contacted by an attorney. All legal and such. Made me sign papers. I'm not actually sure where the money is coming from. I may not be the brightest cowboy in the saddle, but I'm smart enough not to ask."

The line was silent for a moment.

"I'm sorry, Joe. Real sorry. You can see the position this puts me in. I've got a family to consider, as well."

"Sure, I get it, Shady. Don't like it much, but I get it."

Joe stared at the screen. *Money and power.* This was what you could do with enough of each. If that was the case, he'd rather remain a struggling rancher. Maybe it was time to talk to Virginia Simpson.

When the front doorbell rang, Joe realized he'd been

sitting and staring at the screen saver on his monitor for almost ten minutes. Nothing to be accomplished by that.

Yep, he had a problem. That was the beauty of ranch life. No day was ever the same. Pray, then put one foot in front of the other. Deal with it and move on. He closed the laptop and got up to answer the door.

Becca was on his front step with a smile on her face. She'd taken care to conceal her scar and her sutures with a long-sleeve T-shirt.

"Well, look at you," Joe said. "If you didn't have that purple bruise in the middle of your forehead, no one would even guess you got tossed from a horse and scared the life out of me."

"That wasn't exactly my plan for Monday."

"Good to know. So, how do you feel?"

"Oh, I have the expected aches and pains. But I finally figured out how to cover my stitches well enough to wash my hair. I feel one hundred percent better."

"You look good," he said. And she did. Joe itched to reach out and touch the dark hair that flowed around her shoulders.

"Thank you."

"You're not having any headaches or blurred vision?"

"None."

Joe held up his residual limb. The sleeve was folded up and empty. He'd taken off the prosthesis when he came in from the pasture and showered. "How many fingers am I holding up?"

"That's not funny," she said with a frown. "Not one bit."

"Oh, sure it is. If I can't laugh at my own expense, then what's the point? I keep telling you to lighten up, Becca."

"Moving right along." She shook her head. "Abi said you stopped by to talk to me?"

"Yeah. Do you have a minute?"

"Considering that I've done nothing at all but rest today, I've got more than a minute."

"I hate to break it to you," he said with a glance at his watch, "but it's only barely nine a.m. You've only been resting a couple of hours."

"Really? Seems like all day to me. I guess that's because even though you grounded me, I still wake up at three a.m."

Joe chuckled. "Come on in."

"You're all cleaned up on a workday," she noted.

"I had to run some errands in town."

He closed the front door. "Come on down to my office."

"Wait. Let me take off my boots first."

"You don't have to do that."

"I'm not messing up your shiny hardwood floors." She glanced down at the floor and stepped carefully to the side of the entry rug. "Goodness, who cleans this place? You?"

"Hardly. Someone comes in once a week. When I come home it's clean. I write a check and say thank you."

Suddenly Becca's arm flailed in an effort to steady herself. Joe grabbed her hand. The skin was soft to his touch, and an intoxicating whiff of lavender drifted to him.

"Um, thanks," Becca said as she pulled off first one and then the other boot.

He nodded and released her hand.

"Did you get the rest of the cows moved?" she asked as she padded behind him in her stocking feet.

"Cows are safe and sound and grazing happily."

"Good. Good. Oh, and thank you for all you did Monday. Contacting my mother and everything." She hesitated. "I, um, I hope that our talk about, you know… I hope it can remain confidential."

"You don't have to worry. That conversation is on the back burner." He turned and met her gaze. Her brown eyes pleaded with him.

"For the moment," he added.

"Thank you." She breathed the words softly, but there was no mistaking the relief in her voice.

Joe led her into his bookshelf-lined office. He pulled out a chair from the set of sturdy oak chairs that sat on the other side of the desk. "Have a seat."

"It's so tidy in here. It even smells like furniture polish." Her gaze took in the bookshelves that lined several walls, his massive desk and the view of the pasture from the bay window.

"My father's desk used to be piled high with paperwork. I was nearly afraid to go in there."

He tapped his laptop. "It's all in here. If the place seems clean, well, that's because I'm never in here." He pointed out the window. "I'm always out there."

Joe moved to his desk chair. The more distance from Becca the better.

"You wear glasses?" She smiled, her gaze landing on the black frames on his desk.

"Um, yeah." He picked up the glasses and put them away in his drawer. "Paperwork. It makes my eyes cross."

"Sort of Clark Kent, aren't they?"

"Not if you're calling me Superman."

She smiled again, as though the thought amused her.

Joe wished she wouldn't be so perky and bright. Like a candle, she lit up every room she entered.

And here he was, about to throw water on her flame.

She folded her hands in her lap and gave him her full

attention. "So what did you want to talk about? You seem a little tense. Is everything all right?"

"No, it's not. I've been doing a lot of thinking."

"Oh, is something wrong?" Becca swallowed nervously, sat up straight and scooted to the edge of the chair.

"I've decided to send them back to Denver," he announced.

Becca blinked. "Send who? Wh-what?" she sputtered.

"The team from OrthoBorne. This was a crazy idea to start with. One that I take full responsibility for. After all, I'm the one who said yes to this whole thing."

When Becca said nothing, he continued. "You have to admit that it's been nothing short of a domino of disasters. One after another. You getting hurt, well, that was the end of the line for me. I was awake most of last night thinking about this."

"What about certification?" she finally blurted out, her hands gripping the arms of the chair. "You have a contract."

"I'll break it. It's not worth the headache."

"You can't do that. Your prosthesis, you've come so far. Joe, you've actually taught me a few things about using the myoelectric arm. You're going to give up? Now?"

"No. Not at all. I'm not giving up on the arm. You're right. OrthoBorne has given me back much of my freedom, and I'm selfish enough to want to keep it."

"If I can be so bold as to ask, how will you finance the prosthesis?"

"Hollis Elliott," he answered.

"Excuse me?"

"Hollis is interested in a parcel of land that borders his ranch. The man has been nagging me about it for years. I'm going to sell the land to him."

"Gallagher land? Land that's been in your family for, what? Four generations? What will your mother say?"

"My mother only owns a fourth of the ranch. I'm the majority shareholder. I make the decisions, handle the books, and I have since Dad died. She'll see things my way."

Becca shook her head, obviously stunned by the news. "Apparently you've made your decision. I guess there's nothing more to discuss, is there?"

"Not really."

Becca looked past him, her brown eyes glassy. Her gaze was somewhere out the window, far away from the room where they were sitting.

She wiped her palms on her jeans and gave a resigned nod. "I'll break it to the team right away, and we'll clear out. Casey and I will be out of the cottage this weekend."

This time it was Joe who was speechless. "Whoa. No," he finally said. "You and Casey don't have to leave."

"Yes, Joe. We do. I'm part of the certification process, and if you are letting Rod, Julian and Abi go, then naturally, I'll be leaving with the team."

His mind raced. This was not going the way he'd planned. The saddle was definitely being yanked from under him, and he was about to land boots up. It wasn't going to be a pretty sight, either.

"Where will you go?"

"That's not your problem," she said. The words were a slap to his face.

"Call OrthoBorne and see if you can stay."

"Joe, it doesn't work like that. I'm managing your case, and if you are dismissing OrthoBorne, then you are dismissing me, as well."

"I guess I didn't realize…"

"I don't think you've thought any of this through,"

she said. Becca took a deep breath. Her eyes sparked with unspoken frustration. "You're giving up your land… a couple hundred years of Gallagher land, when you could have everything finished up in a few days if we all worked together. Why, pretty much all that's left is for Abi to do her interview. The guys probably have almost enough to finish, as well."

He stared at her. He'd blinked, and the tables had turned.

"It's Thursday night. The sun was shining all day today. That should help your precious hay, right?"

Joe offered a cautious nod, not sure where she was going with the conversation, and he was in too deep to stop now.

"Tomorrow is the Elliott Ranch's Fourth of July barbecue. I'll get them an invitation and send the team to the party. It will keep them off your ranch. They'll have the weekend in town. Come Monday, I'll ride herd on them and get things finished up. They'll be done in twenty-four hours. You have my guarantee."

"I don't know…" Joe hesitated.

"Please, all I'm asking for is the chance to fix this. I've never in my entire life walked away without finishing what I started."

"This isn't about you, Becca."

"Maybe you don't understand what I'm saying. This is very much about me. My reputation is on the line here. I let you down. I let OrthoBorne down. I'm asking… I'm begging for a second chance."

"If I say yes, what about you? What about certification?" he asked.

"I'm sorry, but you know that it will take a bit more time for us to finish. Not much more. You have a DVD to watch and more paperwork. But really, I think we've covered most of the things in the program. I've been going slowly as a courtesy, but I can see that was the wrong approach. I'll speed things up, though I can promise you that I won't disrupt your work. You won't even know I'm around."

"Becca—"

"Hear me out, Joe. You've been angry since I arrived. I understand why. I treated you very badly by walking away without taking the time to talk to you. I was young and so immature. I'm sorry. This is the second time I've apologized, and I won't do it again. I've paid dearly for my choices. Believe me."

"Becca, I keep telling you that you are not the problem."

"Still, I recognize that what you really want is for things to go back to the way they were before. You want normal again."

"Is that what I want?" he murmured, shaking his head.

"Yes, Joe. You've made that abundantly clear in all you say and do. I hardly blame you. It's been disruption after disruption since we arrived. You're right." She nodded. "All I can do is apologize. My job was to liaise, and I've failed miserably."

"No, you haven't." He rubbed his jaw and met her gaze.

"Yes. I have."

"Look, I don't want to argue."

"We aren't arguing. We're discussing," she said.

"Either way. Looks like you have a deal."

"I do?" She turned to meet his gaze, eyes wide.

"Yeah. Let's see where we stand on Monday."

"Thank you," she breathed.

He nodded, more confused than ever.

When Becca stood and walked to the door of his office, he got up from his chair.

She raised a hand and offered him a quick tight smile. "No, don't get up. I can see myself out." Her gaze met his. "You won't regret this. I promise."

So the team would finish up and life would return to normal by as early as Monday night. And that's what he wanted, right?

All along, that was exactly what he'd been saying.

He wanted things to go back to the way they were before the accident.

Joe stared down at his empty sleeve.

Maybe life hadn't been so great before the accident. Maybe the Lord had turned the tragedy of his accident into a blessing. It had brought Becca back into his life, hadn't it?

Joe sat down and leaned back in his chair. Becca back in his life was truly nothing short of a blessing. He liked seeing her smile, especially at four a.m. when he didn't have to share her with anyone but Gil and Wishbone, and the rising sun. He'd grown used to doing chores around the ranch and having someone to talk to besides Blackie. Someone who really understood ranch life. Understood that being a cowboy was only part of it. Being a good stockman and farmer, that was the whole picture.

And what about those snacks? She made something every night since she moved into the cottage—muffins, cookies, whatever—and they'd mysteriously appear in her saddlebag, ready to eat in the middle of the morning when his stomach was rumbling and they were too far from the barn to go back.

Suddenly the way things used to be wasn't half as appealing as the way they were now.

In fact, it was pretty alarming when he thought about it. Life without Becca wasn't much of a life at all.

Chapter Eleven

Abi lifted her fingers from her laptop. Both she and Rod turned from the makeshift worktable in the utility garage to look at Rebecca.

"Did you say we have the rest of the day off?" Rod asked.

"After all the time we lost with the rain, your concussion and the whole Julian cattle fiasco, you're giving us the day off?" Abi asked.

Rebecca smiled. "No, I said you have the rest of the day off *and* you've been invited to the Elliott Ranch annual Fourth of July barbecue."

"Well, that's different. That means sleeping in tomorrow." Rod offered a thumbs-up.

"Must be nice," Rebecca said. "There's a rooster in this part of town. No one sleeps in around here."

"I'm sorry," Abi said.

"Tell us about this barbecue, Rebecca," Rod said as he cleaned his camera lens.

"Sounds like one of those fun small-town events," Abi added.

"Actually," Rebecca said, "it's a pretty big deal around here. Hollis Elliott isn't called the Bison King of Paradise Valley for nothing. Pretty much everyone is on the invitation list, including his cattle and bison cronies. He's been putting on this event at his ranch for as long as I can remember."

"Really?" Abi said.

"Yes. There's always a small country band and all sorts of things to do. They even have rodeo events in the one of the corrals."

"You know," Rod said. "I do some freelance work on the side. This might be a good opportunity to make some connections and add photos to my portfolio."

"There you go. Besides, if nothing else, I can guarantee Mr. Elliott will cater in the best food in the entire valley. Patti Jo's Café and Bakery supplies all the desserts."

"I am so in." Abi grinned.

"Me, too," Rod said. "It was awfully nice of you to get us included. We haven't exactly been candidates for employees of the month since we arrived. I'm pretty sure we've made your life much more challenging."

"He's right. Thank you, Rebecca," Abi added.

"You're welcome. Rod, you were right when you said we're all in the same family. As for Julian, well, I was an intern myself once."

"Please, no one in the history of interns was ever as wet behind the ears as Julian." Rod chuckled. "However, I have to admit. The kid does kind of grow on you after a while."

"He does," Abi admitted. "Like moss."

"The thing is, he means well. You only have a few more days to enjoy his company," Rebecca said. "Monday will be your last day on the ranch. The weather forecast is for sunny skies, with no chance of precipitation. I've promised Mr. Gallagher you will be done by end of day, Monday. So let me know how I can facilitate what you need to complete the project. I intend to keep my word. That means everything must go smoothly on Monday."

Rod shot her a mock salute. "Understood."

"I've got all the background material necessary for my copy. All I need is around thirty minutes with Joe for the actual interview questions," Abi said. "Everything else is gravy. Not that I'm not all about the gravy."

"Rebecca, if you don't mind my asking," Rod said, "why aren't we working today?"

"Um, well, Mr. Gallagher grounded me, due to the concussion. That means the three of you are grounded, too. Sorry about that."

"Certainly not your fault," Abi said.

"Speaking of Julian," Rebecca said glancing around. "Where is our favorite tenderfoot?"

"I sent him to town to get reinforcements from Patti Jo's," Abi said. "We were out of cookies."

"Was that wise? Setting him loose on a defenseless town?" Rod asked.

"He'll be fine," Abi returned with a wave of her hand. "I'd like to stress that I really needed a Patti Jo fix."

Rebecca smiled at the exchange as she started toward the cottage.

"Hey, wait up," Abi asked, jogging to catching up to her. "What about you?"

"Me?"

"You're going to the barbecue?" Abi asked.

"Sure. I'm excited. I haven't been in over a dozen years. It'll be fun to show Casey the Elliott Ranch. I was pretty much raised there."

"Is your mom going?"

"Mr. Elliott sent her a personal invitation."

"Ooh! What's going on there?"

Rebecca shook her head. "I'm not sure."

"That sounds like a romance-tell to me."

"What do you mean? Romance-tell?"

"You know, those little gestures a guy makes that show he cares when he doesn't have the courage to actually say something. Like Joe does around you."

"I'm going to ignore that. But I think you might be right about Hollis Elliott. Except that it's my mother, so maybe I really don't want to know."

Abi stopped walking and her eyes rounded.

"What?" Rebecca asked.

"I just realized you said pretty much everyone will be there. Does that mean my favorite sheriff will be in attendance?"

"Eventually. He's got his hands full on the fourth. There's a big parade in downtown Paradise in the morning. The Paradise Sheriff's Department consists of one full-time sheriff and deputy, and a few part-timers, plus the administrative assistant. They'll be stretched pretty thin."

"I imagine Casey would like to go to the parade. I'd be more than happy to take her. Of course you'd have to lend me your car."

Rebecca chuckled. "We can all go."

They both made their way back to the cottage. Rebecca peeked in the door to check on her mother and Casey before taking a seat on one of the wide steps outside.

They were silent for moments before Abi turned to her. "I assume the boss found you?"

"Yes." Rebecca shook her head, remembering her conversation with Joe.

"You've got a lot riding on this whole project, don't you?" Abi said quietly.

"I do."

"I don't mean just the bonus," Abi said.

Rebecca's head jerked back, and she met Abi's gaze. "How do you know about the bonus?"

"I'm a writer. It's my job to be a fly on the wall. I pay very close attention to details. Though in reality, I have to admit that I heard it around the office before I left."

"You haven't told anyone, have you?"

"Do I look indiscreet?"

She raised her brows. "I don't know you well enough to make that call."

"We all have our secrets, and I've learned the hard way that God gave us two ears and one mouth for a very good reason. If you'll recall, when I first arrived I said that I'd read about you, yet I've never mentioned it."

"That's true and I appreciate that."

"You can trust me, Rebecca—however, I'm guessing that if I know, Rod and Julian do, as well."

"Really?"

She nodded. "But what does that matter? You deserve the bonus. OrthoBorne really wants Gallagher for this campaign, and you're delivering the goods. It's a nobrainer that you've earned it. You're up before all of us. You finesse everyone's needs before your own. This project will be a success because of you. Good grief, taming the lion alone deserves a bonus."

"What lion?"

Abi chuckled. "You know. Grumpy Gallagher."

"Is that what you call him?" Rebecca released a small gasp. "Oh, he's not—"

"Oh, yes, he is. Though things have sort of changed. He hardly ever growls around you since you were thrown by that horse."

"I'm not sure what you mean."

"Surely you are aware that Joe Gallagher cares a great deal about you."

"We have history. We were friends for a long time, Abi."

Abi shook her head. "Rebecca, this is much more than friendship."

Rebecca froze at the words. She glanced around, concerned someone might overhear. "What on earth makes you think that?" she whispered.

"You didn't see his face when you were thrown from Princess. Anguish. It was as though a part of him was dying." Abi nodded. "I'd like someone to get that worked up over me." She sighed, resting her chin on her hand.

"I think you're looking at the world through a writer's glasses."

"I admit that can be a side effect of my job. Except not in this case. No." She shook her head. "Gallagher wears his heart on his sleeve. It's obvious to everyone, with the exception of Julian. Big surprise there."

"How can it be obvious to everyone, when it seems quite the opposite to me?" Rebecca paused, remembering how Joe had shied away the one time she thought he might kiss her.

"Maybe because, as you said, you've known him a long time. So you haven't noticed how things have shifted."

"It's true we go way back. The fact is, I sort of, well..." Rebecca grimaced. "I dumped him a long time ago."

"Not one of your better decisions, I imagine."

Rebecca turned her head slowly and stared at Abi. She'd certainly nailed it. "I was young and naive like Julian. I was swept off my feet by Nick, and no, dumping Joe wasn't one of my finer moments. Except that now I have Casey, who's the best thing I've done with my life so far."

"If I'm right and Joe does have feelings for you, are you telling me that you don't have any for him?"

"I haven't spent a lot of time thinking about it." Rebecca looked away. "We're working together long hours. That's part of the job. Don't get me wrong, I like Joe, but the timing couldn't be more wrong."

"Life is like that, I hear. It happens at the most inconvenient times."

Rebecca pondered the truth of Abi's blithe response.

"Why is it you do so much ranch work?" Abi asked as she leaned back on her elbows.

"I like doing ranch work." Rebecca frowned at the random question.

"You don't have to get up every day and help Joe with the chores. He's been doing them without you for years."

"His certification."

Abi leveled her with a look that said "try again."

"I said I like ranch work."

"Do you like ranch work, or do you like ranch work with Joe?"

"You're really pushing my buttons here, aren't you, Ms. Reporter?" Rebecca huffed.

"Well?" Abi prodded.

"Good question. I'll have to get back to you."

"You might want to think long and hard before you ignore what's right in front of you."

"Spoken like someone who's been there?"

Abi chuckled and stretched out her hands, examining her nails with a frown. "Sure. Everyone has a story. But the truth is, I really like you, Rebecca. I don't want you to make the same mistake I did."

Rebecca sighed. "I've made so many, what's one more?"

"Is Joe going to the barbecue?"

"I forgot to ask. I was too busy trying to save our project."

"What do you mean?" Abi sat up straight.

"Joe was ready to throw in the towel."

"Is that why he was looking for you?"

Rebecca nodded.

"Why didn't you tell us it was this serious?"

"I didn't want to worry you."

Abi took a deep breath. "You've got a lot riding on Monday. Bringing this project in will make us all look good. We're in the homestretch now, thanks to you. Don't worry. I'll do my part to make sure the guys stay on task."

"Thank you. No need to mention any of this to Rod and Julian."

"I won't. Of course they're going to wonder why I suddenly show up with a cattle prod Monday morning."

Rebecca laughed. "I wish I'd thought of that."

A horn double tooted, announcing a car's arrival, and Rebecca and Abi looked up.

"Julian is back," Abi drawled with a hint of pain in her voice.

"We're going to have to discuss the top ten reasons why you don't lay on the horn when you live on a ranch."

"You can take the kid out of the city…" Abi said.

Rebecca just shook her head.

"Look, Momma. I can see the flags." Casey jumped up and down in her seat, barely restrained by the car's seat belt.

A morning at the Fourth of July parade in downtown Paradise hadn't dimmed her enthusiasm or her energy.

Rebecca followed her daughter's gaze out the car window to the Elliott Ranch. Banners with the ranch logo, and red, white and blue flags all waved in the afternoon breeze. Neighbors from the valley were moving through the huge black iron *E* archway of the ranch to the festivities. The peppy twang of a country band could be heard playing a familiar Western tune in the distance. Rebecca could hardly resist toe tapping.

"Okay, Casey, here's the rules. This is a huge ranch. I must know where you are at all times, and you must always be with an adult. Either me, or Grandma or Abi. Got it?"

Casey nodded.

"Are Julian and Rod riding out together?" Rebecca asked Abi who was in the passenger seat.

"Yes. And if we're really lucky they'll get lost."

"Abi."

"Please, Julian could single-handedly ruin this shindig," Abi said as she slathered sunscreen on her bare arms.

"Be kind."

"I can deny I know him," Abi said. "Would that be implausible deniability?" She laughed at her own joke as she straightened the skirt of her sundress.

"Cute dress," Rebecca said, noting Abi's outfit with its little shrug sweater.

"If I had one of those pretty embroidered, yoked Western shirts like yours, I would have gone cowgirl, too. Must remedy that."

"Momma, is Joe here yet? He told me he'd take me on a pony ride. Does he count as an adult?"

Abi stifled a laugh with a hand over her mouth.

"Yes. He does." She looked at her daughter. "Joe told you he was coming?"

Casey nodded.

"Oh, look, Casey, they're painting faces over there. Rebecca, do you mind if I take her over?"

"Sure, go ahead, I'm going to look for Sara, Mr. Elliott's daughter. I can't wait to see her twins. Come and find me when you two are done."

Abi took Casey's hand. "We will, but you might not recognize us, right, Casey?"

Casey giggled.

Rebecca took her time strolling across the grass, nodding at the few people she did know, most of them friends of her mother's. There was a time when she knew every single person in Paradise, along with every inch of this ranch, just like her father. But those days were long gone. She often wondered what would have happened if her father was still here?

How strange it seemed to be back. Ten years ago she'd just graduated from high school. She and Joe had gone to that summer's barbecue together. It was her first year to attend without her father. Joe had been so caring. Moving to town after her father's death had been tough. Coming back to the ranch, her home for most of her life, as an outsider for the first time had been even more difficult.

Yet Joe had been there when she needed a friend. Then a mere two years later their worlds had parted.

"Whoa, careful there, Becca, you almost ran me over."

He looked good—too good to be loose at a party where there was a thirty-to-one ratio of women to men. He wore a crisp white fancy yoked Western shirt with pearl buttons and red embroidery, along with well-worn creased Levi's and his tan Stetson.

"Joe. Casey said you were coming today."

"Good opportunity to chat with Hollis," Joe said.

"I thought you were going to give us until Monday night."

"I am."

In the silence that followed, the tension between them became palpable.

"I don't like this," Joe said, his jaw set. "Not one bit."

"What do you mean?"

"This." When he gestured with both of his hands, instead of just one, Rebecca was so happy to see she'd finally made significant progress with his therapy.

She smiled.

"Hey, where'd you go? Did you hear what I said?" Joe said.

"Yes. I was smiling at your bilateral use of your hands. We therapists call that significant progress."

"You therapists are a strange bunch."

"Perhaps. What was it you were grumbling about?"

He put on his Joe scowl and shoved a hand in his pocket. "I was about to apologize for being testy lately."

"I thought that was normal."

"Are you being funny?"

"No, I'm simply agreeing that you've been rather cranky since the team and I arrived."

His head jerked back slightly. "Well, don't hold back. Why did you suddenly decide to tell me this?"

"I was agreeing with you. I'm glad you brought it up, though. You and I should clear the air since my time at the ranch is almost over."

"I'd like it if we could be friends," Joe admitted.

"Me, too."

"Good." He gave a satisfied nod. "Wow. Smell that?" Joe took a deep breath, inhaling the savory barbecue aroma that hung in the summer air. "I've got to get some of that. Have you eaten?"

"No. I was waiting for Casey and Abi. They're face painting."

"How about we grab a little something while you're waiting?"

"Yes, sure." She smiled up at him, and it occurred to her that there was nothing else she'd rather do right now. She couldn't change the past, but creating a future with Joe as her friend would be a very nice thing.

"Perfect day, isn't it?" Joe asked.

"It is," Rebecca returned, trying to match her strides with his.

He stopped. "Hold it. What am I doing? I clean forgot."

"Forgot what?" She turned around when she realized he was no longer next to her.

"I ordered something for you, and it showed up yesterday."

"You did?" She glanced up at him. "Why?"

"Because you need it, and after the week you've had, you've earned it." He did an about-face and took off in the other direction.

"Wait," Rebecca called as she struggled to keep up.

"Come on." He stopped and reached for her hand. Rebecca held on tight.

"I'm parked right over there."

She followed, weaving around the sea of pickup trucks that left no doubt that this was an agricultural community.

"Here it is." Joe reached into his flatbed and pulled out a hat can.

"You got me a hat?"

"Yeah. I told you that you need one. This beauty is a Stetson with a pinch-front crown." He unclipped the can and opened it.

Rebecca gasped. "It's the prettiest hat I've ever seen." She ran a hand over the smooth fur felt.

"I figured you can get your own band when you have time." He gently lifted it from the box.

"How did you know what size?"

"They still have you on file in the store."

"Wow, after all these years. I don't even know where my old hats are. Maybe in my mother's attic."

"Well, aren't you going to try it on?"

"Yes. Of course." She rubbed her hand over the taupe material. "I love the color."

"Thought this color wouldn't show the dirt in case you, um, fall again."

"That wasn't my fault."

"I'm just saying."

"Your hat matches mine." Delighted with the hat, she placed it on her head and adjusted the brim.

"Does it?"

Rebecca glanced at him and he winked.

"How's it look?" she asked, moving to the side-view mirror of the truck."

"Careful."

Too late, Rebecca tripped on an orange plastic traffic cone lying on its side in the grass.

Joe grabbed her around the waist, alarm in his eyes.

"You almost fell. Do you have any idea how dangerous a concussion is? Everything from dazed and confused, to full-on memory loss. Hitting your head when you already have a concussion is even more dangerous. You've got to be more cautious, Becca."

She narrowed her eyes, assessing him. "When did you get a medical degree?"

Joe gave a sheepish smile and shrugged. "I looked it up on WebMD."

"You looked up my concussion?"

"Yeah, about midnight, when I couldn't sleep. I was worried about you."

Rebecca stood still in the warm circle of his arms as he stared at her. His gaze moved from her eyes to her lips. Then ever so slowly, Joe's head lowered. He hesitated and stepped back, releasing her.

"Sorry," he murmured. "I shouldn't start what I can't finish. We only just became friends again, five minutes ago. I don't want to make it any more difficult than it is."

"Difficult? What's difficult?"

"I'm doing my best to maintain a professional relationship, but you sure aren't making it easy."

"Me!"

"It would help if you could ugly yourself up or something."

Rebecca snickered. "Doesn't this black-and-blue knot in the middle of my forehead work for you?"

"Not hardly," he scoffed. "Besides, you're assigned to certify me. It would be wrong to attempt to unduly sway your opinion."

Though she did her best, Rebecca couldn't help but laugh. Repeatedly. "Are you saying you think I might go ahead and certify you because you're a good kisser?"

Joe's face registered shock. "No. That is not what I'm saying."

She shook her head. "I'm kidding, Joe. Let's just go get something to eat, shall we?"

"Sure. Okay. But take it easy today, would you?"

"I'll try," she said. "Slowing down doesn't come naturally for me."

"Where have you two been?" Abi murmured to Rebecca as they approached the root beer table. She looked her up and down. "Nice hat."

"Mr. Gallagher decided that I need one." She looked

at Joe. "Or maybe he buys one for every greenhorn who gets thrown by a horse on his ranch."

Abi laughed, and Joe shot the reporter a menacing stare.

"How do you like my face, Joe?" Casey asked.

"Red, white and blue with stars. I like it. Maybe I should get a few stars, too."

"Casey, you are beautiful," Rebecca said.

"How about if we go check out those ponies, Casey?" Joe asked.

"I thought you were hungry," Rebecca said.

"Yeah, not anymore," he mumbled.

"Are Momma and Abi coming, too?"

He shook his head. "Nope. Just you and me. That okay?"

Casey's face lit up. "Yes, please."

Joe took her hand, and they headed off to find the ponies.

"Oh, my. Look at them," Abi said, her gaze following the tall cowboy and the little girl. "That's enough to make even my cynical heart a little mushy around the edges."

Rebecca chuckled. "He's a good man."

"Ditto that.

"So you and Joe looked cozy." Abi raised her brows. "I am going to make a wild guess that he's forgiven you for bringing us out to the ranch?"

"Yes. At least for today. Monday will be the real test."

"Rebecca. Good to see you," a voice behind her said.

She turned and smiled, delighted to see Hollis Elliott. He wore a black Western shirt and a black hat angled on the back of his head. The outfit offset his thick white shock of hair. "Mr. Elliott! How wonderful to see you." She gave him a quick hug.

"Sir, this is Abigail Warren, she's here as part of the

OrthoBorne Technology team, doing a big write-up on Mr. Gallagher."

"Pleased to meet you."

"You as well, sir. This is an amazing community event. Thank you for allowing us to attend."

"Glad you're here. Paradise gives me so much. This is my way of giving back. Enjoy yourself."

He turned to Rebecca. "Do you mind if I steal you away from your friend for a few moments?"

"Abi?"

"Of course. As it happens, I have a sheriff I'd like to have a word with." She grinned.

"What happened to your forehead?" he asked, peering at her face.

"Thrown from a horse, like I was a rookie. So embarrassing."

Hollis chuckled. "Well, you know what they say. 'If you climb in the saddle, be ready for the ride.' Not that I haven't been tossed a couple times. It's all about how you land, right?"

"Yes, sir." Rebecca smiled, recalling that her father had said those same words.

"Let me get down to business, so you can get back to having fun. I wanted to apologize to you, Rebecca. I found out too late what Judge Brown was trying to do to you with that trial. Next time he bothers you, come to me. That windbag doesn't have as much reach as he thinks he does. I'm only sorry your momma didn't call me first when you needed bail money. And for the record, I knew all along you were innocent. Everyone in this town did."

"Thank you, Mr. Elliott. You were a lifesaver, believe me."

"Nonsense. It would have been the least I could do for your father."

"Sir, could I possibly ask a small favor?"

"Anything, Rebecca."

"Joe Gallagher."

"What about him?"

"Judge Brown has managed to prevent him from hiring help with his hay crop, because I'm working with him. I'm his therapist."

"I just talked to Gallagher. He didn't say anything about that. We talked about his land. There's a parcel I've been trying to get him to sell. That's a standing joke between us. Has been for years. That boy will never sell. He likes to tease me every now and again. Someday he plans to build a house on that parcel and raise a big family."

Rebecca frowned, confused.

"When does Joe start cutting?" Hollis asked.

"Tuesday. Next week will be the first full week of sunshine we've had."

"You're right. Everyone is scrambling to get in the first cutting. I've got my balers tied up with my crop at the moment, but I'm not willing to let the judge get away with this. No, sir. It's not right. Let me see what I can figure out."

"I appreciate that, sir."

"Don't you worry." He grinned and patted her back. "I'll beat the judge at his own game. I'm good at that."

"Thank you."

"I don't suppose your mother is here?"

"She should be somewhere around here. I spoke to her before I left. She was bringing a few of the elderly ladies from the church."

"Your mother is a good woman. Heart of gold. A godly woman, as well."

"Yes, sir, she is."

"Do you mind if I ask you a personal question?"

Rebecca shook her head.

"Would it bother you if I…" He hesitated and cleared his throat as a red flush crept up his neck. "I'd like to ask your mother out to dinner."

She smiled. "That would be really nice."

"You're sure? I don't want to overstep my bounds. The way I figure it, your mother's been widowed fourteen years, and my dear wife has been gone twenty. I'd like nothing more than conversation and a meal now and again, with a lovely lady who understands ranching and cares about this valley as much as I do."

"You don't need my permission, Mr. Elliott. But if you feel you do, you have it."

"Thank you." He grinned. His dark eyes had a definite spark in them. "Now have a good time today. We won't do this again until next year."

Rebecca stood with a smile on her face as Hollis moved to greet his guests and check on the events. Her mother deserved a second chance at companionship, and maybe a little romance. Deserved it more than anyone she knew. Her heart swelled with joy at the possibilities that lay ahead for all of them here in Paradise.

Chapter Twelve

Rebecca curled her feet beneath her and relaxed against the leather sofa. "What did you think of our little church, Abi?"

"I have to admit that it was a pleasant surprise. Everything. The sermon, the people. It's been a long time since I've sat in a pew."

"Any particular reason?" Rebecca asked.

"Oh, lots of reasons. None of them of any merit." Abi paused and turned her head. "Before you start digging into my psyche, I should mention that I think that's your phone ringing."

Rebecca scrambled from the couch and raced to her room. Dumping the contents of her purse on the bed, she rifled through an assortment of papers along with souvenirs from Friday's barbecue. When had Casey have time to put all this stuff in her purse? Finally, at the bottom of everything, she located her cell.

Virginia Simpson. She tapped "accept" when she saw the familiar number.

"Virginia?"

"I know this is short notice, Rebecca—however, a situation has arisen here. I'm leaving for Denver late tonight.

Could you possibly come up to the house? I've wanted to talk to you for a long time. Now I find that I cannot put it off any longer."

Rebecca blinked, speechless for a moment at the unexpected request. "Um, yes. Sure. No problem. I'm happy to take a ride up there."

"When? Would now be too inconvenient?"

"Now?" Rebecca glanced at the clock at her bedside. "Okay. I'll make it work. Um, your father? Will he be there?"

"No. The judge isn't here." Virginia paused. "When shall I expect you?"

"I'll leave right away. Give me a few minutes to make arrangements for Casey. She's sleeping, and I don't want to wake her."

Rebecca ended the call and stared at her cell for a moment before dropping it, her wallet and car keys back into her purse. Something niggled at her. What was she forgetting?

The judge.

She tensed when she realized that she hadn't received any harassing calls from Judge Brown in several days. Did that, along with the fact that Virginia had summoned her out of the blue, mean something?

Admittedly, talking to Virginia was something she'd been meaning to do for a long time. Meaning to and avoiding. How was she going explain to her former mother-in-law that the woman's father was harassing her? Who would believe that an elderly respected community member spent his spare time prank dialing her? Were the calls even actionable?

It didn't matter. Virginia should know. It was time. Time to take back her life. Time to move forward.

Rebecca glanced down at her navy church dress. She

pulled up the sleeve and took a long look at the disfiguring scar. Next to the healing sutures Sara had given her, the scar seemed especially ugly and mocking. Opening the closet, she yanked a short-sleeve blouse from a hanger, along with a pair of slacks.

She changed her clothes and stood looking at herself in the full-length mirror. No more hiding. The scar had been her secret for too long. Sara was right; the scar needed to be revised. A lot of things in her life were ready and waiting to be revised.

Sliding her feet into flats, she shoved everything back into her purse before closing her bedroom door.

"Abi, I hate to ask you a favor on your day off—"

"Please," Abi interrupted. "Ask away. I owe you plenty, and you made that wonderful lunch."

"Would you mind watching Casey for me for a few hours? That was her other grandmother on the phone. She asked me to stop by, and it's about a twenty-minute drive each way."

"Of course. That's a pretty easy favor. Take your time." Abi waved a hand and continued to type on her laptop. "I'm working on the piece about Joe. I want to have it ready for his approval tomorrow. This is good stuff, if I do say so myself. I think I might submit a feature article to the *Denver Post*, as well. With his permission, of course."

"I don't want to burst your bubble, but Joe splashed all over the Denver paper probably isn't going to excite him."

Abi sighed. "I suspected as much."

"You have my cell number, right?"

She nodded.

"Casey's still napping," Rebecca said.

"I meant what I said. Take your time. We'll play board games when she wakes up."

"Thanks, Abi."

Rebecca grabbed a bottle of water from the fridge and headed out the door.

"I was just looking for you."

Rebecca looked up, surprised to see Joe. He was smiling as he strode toward her. Smiling had to be a good sign. Right?

She offered a cautious smile in return, not sure what the protocol was after spending the day together yesterday. "You okay?" he asked.

"Yes."

"What do you think about you, me and Casey heading to Patti Jo's for a late lunch?"

"I wish I could. Virginia Simpson has summoned me to the castle. I'm leaving now."

"That explains why you look so tense." He paused. "I'm not doing anything else. I'll drive you."

"You don't have to do that." She unlocked the Honda.

He shot her a steely gaze. "I'll drive you."

"Why?"

"Sometimes we need backup."

"Oh?"

"Sure. The Lone Ranger and Tonto. Butch Cassidy and the Sundance Kid. Kirk and Spock. Han Solo and Chewbacca."

"Bert and Ernie?"

Joe laughed. "Exactly. I'm starting to realize how much we're alike, Becca. Most of our problems in life stem from our inability to ask for help when we need it."

Her eyes rounded. "Excuse me?"

"You heard me. Speaking as one stubborn cowboy to another, you have to recognize when you need reinforcement. You can't be afraid to ask for help, and you can't be afraid to accept it."

She gingerly massaged the tender spot on her forehead. The only thing she recognized at the moment was that the idea of meeting with Virginia had already given her a headache. "Okay, I'm too stressed to argue, especially when there's a possibility you might be right."

"Of course I am." He nodded toward the barn. "Now wait right here, Ernie, and I'll get my truck."

"You sure have been quiet," Joe said once they arrived in Four Forks.

"Sorry. A lot on my mind," Rebecca returned.

"Do you know why she wants to see you?" Joe asked as he guided the truck up the mountain road to the Simpson home.

"No clue," she murmured. "And I don't mind telling you that alone makes me nervous."

"That's an understatement. You've been staring out the window and sighing for the last twenty minutes."

"Have I, really?"

He nodded. "Hey, look at that. Smiley is back on duty. The gate is even open. I guess he's expecting you." Joe gave the sour-faced guard a friendly wave as they passed by the security booth.

He drove the truck around the circle drive to the front door, where he unbuckled his seat belt.

"Joe, this time you have to wait in the truck."

"I can do that. I'll park over there, by the tennis courts."

"Okay." She glanced at the house and then away several times, attempting to bolster her courage.

She could do this. She could do this.

"Rebecca?"

"Hmm?"

"You know that promise you wanted me to keep?"

"Yes?" She said the word slowly.

"I know this won't be easy, but it's time for you to take care of what you wouldn't let me take care of."

She gave a quick nod "You're right. I know you're right. I'm going to tell her everything. I'm going to move forward."

"You can do this, Becca."

"Can I? If I wasn't such a coward, I would have taken care of this years ago."

"You're doing it now. That's what matters." Joe stared at her and frowned. "You look like you're going to pass out. I think we better say a quick prayer." He took her hand and held it against his heart. "Lord, give Becca the words to say today. Guide her and protect her. Amen."

Rebecca leaned forward and pressed a soft kiss to his cheek. "Thank you," she whispered.

"Ah, you're welcome."

He came around and opened the passenger door and helped her down. "Remember. I've got your back."

"You and God. Yes. You're right. She nodded and walked slowly past the high columns to the generously proportioned front door.

Virginia answered on the first knock. She was unsmiling, and she seemed even more solemn than usual. There was something weighing heavily on her mind. She glanced from Rebecca to Joe's truck. "Thank you for coming."

Rebecca clutched her purse tightly as Virginia ushered her into the large entrance way. Her heels echoed on the marble floor.

"Did you fall?" Virginia looked from Rebecca's forehead to her arm. "Oh, my. Stitches, as well?"

"I was thrown from a horse.

"You're riding again?"

"I am. Not well, apparently."

Virginia frowned. "How unfortunate."

"Part and parcel," Rebecca murmured.

"Shall we sit in the living room?" Virginia asked.

"That's fine."

She looked quickly around as they passed from the entrance, through French doors and into the living room. Even after all these years, very little had changed in the room from the days when she and Nick would visit his family. He'd been an up-and-coming legal prodigy, mentored by his grandfather. But the pressure of meeting his grandfather's expectations seemed to be the catalyst that started spinning Nick's life out of control. They stopped visiting Four Forks. Nick rarely did anything, but work. He hardly noticed that he had a wife and a child.

Virginia smoothed her white linen slacks as she perched on the silk brocade couch. With a hand, she beckoned for Rebecca to sit next to her.

"I thought maybe it was time for us to discuss the future," Virginia said.

"The future? Whose future?"

"Casey's. Yours. Mine."

Rebecca nodded. She folded her hands in her lap and took a deep breath. "I hope you understand that before I can deal with the future, I need to deal with the past."

"I meant it when I said I knew you were innocent, Rebecca. I can't apologize enough for what my father put you through. What I allowed."

"That's not what I meant." She glanced around, praying she still had the courage to do what must finally be done. "Where did you say Judge Brown is?"

"He's in Denver. My father had a stroke yesterday morning. That's one of the reasons I wanted to talk to you."

"Oh." Rebecca froze. "How's he doing?"

"Please keep him in your prayers. I know it seems as though he doesn't deserve them, but he needs them. He's lost most of the use of his right side. His doctors have told me that full recovery is doubtful. With his other medical issues, we're hoping to keep him comfortable in a facility in Denver until his condition stabilizes and we can decide what's next."

"I see. What do you want me to tell Casey?"

"Nothing for now. I was in Denver all day yesterday. Jana is with him now. I'm closing out the house and will leave tonight."

"Maybe this isn't the time for us to talk. I don't want to add to your stress. You have a lot going on."

"I think we've put this off for far too long."

Rebecca nodded. "You're right."

"I now have power of attorney for my father's estate. I discovered he's been harassing you. His lawyer tells me he's been harassing Joseph Gallagher, as well." Virginia shook her head. "I wish you would have told me."

"I couldn't."

"Trust me, it will stop. Immediately."

"Thank you."

"Tell me about my son." Virginia took a deep breath and met Rebecca's gaze. "I haven't wanted to know. It's taken me two years, and I'm finally ready to face the truth. Nick had a drinking problem like his father. That much I am sure of."

Rebecca hesitated. Was Virginia really prepared for what she had to say?

"Nick… Nick was an alcoholic. When he drank, he became physically and verbally abusive. Never in front of his daughter." Rebecca held her hands tightly in her lap, her nails biting into her skin, as she admitted the truth aloud. A truth she had never revealed to anyone before.

"Oh, no, no." Virginia's words were a soft painful wail. She covered her mouth with her hands and closed her eyes. "You poor child."

"Nick often got a little carried away." She unfolded her hands and moved her fingers over the rough scar.

Virginia's gaze moved to Rebecca's arm and her face paled.

"That's what he would say. 'I got a little carried away. I didn't mean it.'" Rebecca swallowed. "This scar…it's from one of the times when he got a little carried away."

Silent tears ran down Virginia's cheeks. "I think I've suspected as much all along, which makes me as guilty as my son." She raised her face. "Nick made you lose control of the car, didn't he?"

Rebecca nodded. "Nick was furious because I took the car keys after he'd obviously had too much to drink. He took off his seat belt and grabbed the wheel." This time she closed her eyes, remembering that horrible night. It happened in an instant. The car had veered off the road, skidded as she fought for control of the wheel, and finally crashed. Then everything had been very silent, the only sound was the rain tapping on the windshield.

"I'm sorry," Rebecca whispered. The apology was for Virginia and maybe for Nick, as well.

She raised her head and met Virginia's gaze. "More sorry than you know. I should have demanded that he get help long ago."

"We can't fix people. You couldn't fix Nick. I couldn't fix his father." She wiped her tears and sniffed. "Yet you never told anyone."

"No. For years I believed it was my fault. My secret.

My shame. It's taken a long time for me to understand that was wrong thinking."

"Why didn't your lawyer use this information in court?"

"I wouldn't let him. This was my daughter's father, and I honestly believed, deep down inside, that the guilt was mine. Those were the darkest days of my life, until I finally turned everything over to God."

"My father needs to know."

"You're the only one who can talk to your father. I can't do that to him. I doubt if he'd believe me anyhow."

"This just might destroy him. Nick was everything to the judge."

"There was a time when he was everything to me, too."

"Who's that man who drove you here?"

"That's Joe Gallagher."

"May I ask how he fits into your life? Into Casey's?"

"I don't know. I'm rebuilding my life one day at a time. Joe's a good man, a good friend, but I don't know what the future holds."

"The Lord brought you back here for a reason, Rebecca. Stay close to Him. Don't throw away your second chance."

"I won't."

"Thank you for shielding Casey." She took Rebecca's hand in hers. "You sacrificed yourself for your daughter."

"I'd do it again in a heartbeat. Casey is the best of Nick and me. I see him in her all the time. She has his sense of humor, and she's smart. Smarter than both Nick and I. Maybe she'll grow up to be a lawyer."

"Or maybe she'll be a rancher. A horsewoman, like her mother," Virginia said.

"Whatever she wants to be. Casey has a full life ahead of her."

"Thank you. Thank you for telling me the truth. Despite everything, you've given us another chance. I'm grateful."

"I want to live in Paradise. I want Casey to grow up with a close relationship with her father's family. Do you think we can do that?"

"Yes. I want the same things."

Rebecca stood alone on the steps of the Simpson home and took a deep, cleansing breath as she looked around, almost expecting the world to have changed.

It had. Things were different, she realized. For the first time in a very long time she was free from the secrets of her past. The accident could no longer hold her hostage, nor could the awful memories.

Up ahead, Joe stood next to the truck, waiting for her. He was a good man and what Virginia said echoed in her head. The Lord had given her a second chance and she was going to do everything she could to hold onto it.

"How'd it go?" He moved to open her door. Taking her arm, he helped her step up into the cab of the truck and waited for her answer, concern on his face.

"That was probably the hardest thing I've ever done in my life. It was like burying Nick all over again. Yet it was also about forgiving him and saying goodbye to the past. I can finally close the door." She released a breath and leaned back against the seat. "I'm exhausted."

"What about the judge?"

"He won't bother either of us again."

"Becca, I'm so proud of you."

"You know what? I'm proud of me, too."

Rebecca nodded toward the packet on Joe's desk.

"This is it. We're finished, right?" Joe asked with a smile.

"We're finished as soon as you sign off on the photos and the video clips."

"I did."

"The write-up Abi did, too?"

"All signed and dated." He grinned and handed the stack to her.

"I'll take it back to Rod and Abi."

"No more 'turn slightly to the left, Mr. Gallagher.' 'Hold those reins with your right hand, Mr. Gallagher.' 'Give us a smile for the camera. Chin up. Hold that pose.'"

She raised a brow. "Now you're plain exaggerating. It wasn't that bad."

"Yeah, it was."

Rebecca cleared her throat. She frowned, trying to figure out the best way to broach the next subject.

"Okay, now what's wrong?" he asked.

"The team wants to talk to you."

"Say goodbye and all?"

"Um, not exactly."

"What exactly does 'not exactly' mean?"

"They're outside. Maybe I should let them explain."

"Oh, no." Joe shook his head and groaned. "I've got a real bad feeling about this, Becca. Can't you give me a heads-up?"

"It's not my place."

His shoulders sank. "Okay, Fine. Bring them in."

Joe offered a weak smile as the rest of the OrthoBorne team filed into his office.

Rod stepped forward. "Mr. Gallagher, we've been talking."

Joe's eyes rounded. He swallowed.

"We've decided to stay."

"Come again?" He blinked and shot a "help me" look at Rebecca.

"We're going to harvest the hay with you. It's the least we can do for all you've put up with."

Joe raised both hands. "That's not necessary."

"It is," Rod said. "Rebecca told us you're having a hard time getting help." He looked at Abi and Julian and smiled. "We're here and we're free. You can't hardly beat a deal like that, even in Paradise."

He turned to her again. "You told them?"

"It sort of came up in conversation," Rebecca said.

Joe opened his mouth and closed it. He scratched his head. Finally he looked up at Rod. "What do you know about cutting and baling hay?"

"I watched about a dozen videos on YouTube this morning. Today, I went out to the barn to inspect your equipment. I don't see any reason why I couldn't relieve you on the windrower. I used to work in the garden department of my local greenhouse. I've worked a forklift many times. Not much difference between that and your skid loader."

"Gotta love the internet." Joe chuckled.

"Especially WebMD," Rebecca muttered.

When Joe jerked his head around to look at her, she realized there was a good chance that pushing his buttons might not be the best approach.

"So how long after you cut are you going to bale?" Rod asked.

"We've had a run of good weather. Counting today, we've had four days of sunshine. The hay is prime for cutting. The forecast is in our favor. Humidity is back to normal, which is next to nothing in Colorado. You can't do better than cut one day, rake and bale the next. We're just going to give it our best shot."

"We?" Rod asked.

"I'm probably out of my mind." Joe scratched his head. "But I'm considering taking you up on your offer."

"That's great," Rod said. He offered a grin filled with enthusiasm.

"I'd like to help, as well. What can I do?" Abi asked with a smile.

"Well, um…" Joe swallowed.

"Never mind. I'll stand around and look good. That should be plenty."

Rebecca laughed. "Oh, I can think of a dozen chores you and I can do while Joe is cutting hay. No worries. I'll make you a list, and then get you the keys to the truck."

"I can cook," Julian said quietly.

"What did you say?" Rebecca asked.

"I said, I can cook."

"Since when?" Abi asked, surprise lacing her voice.

"I attended Le Cordon Bleu College of Culinary Arts in Scottsdale on full scholarship."

"Wh-what?" Abi sputtered.

"Why are you working at OrthoBorne?" Rod asked.

"It pays better."

Joe's cell phone rang and he raised a palm to silence the room. "Yes, sir… Yes, sir… Looks like Wednesday, possibly Thursday, as well." He paused, blinked and then raised his brows in stunned surprise. "Yes, sir. Thank you."

He turned slowly to stare at Rebecca. "That was Hollis Elliott. When we're ready, he'll send over a team with equipment to rake and bale."

"A team?" she asked slowly.

"That's what the man said. Do you know anything about this?" he asked.

Rebecca shrugged and glanced away. "I might have mentioned that you were baling."

"That's all?"

"Hollis is a generous man."

"Yeah, right."

"Well, Joe," Rebecca said with a wink, "speaking as one stubborn cowboy to another, you have to recognize when you need backup. You can't be afraid to ask for help and you can't be afraid to accept it."

Joe gave a nod of approval, a slow smile appearing on his lips as if he recalled saying those same words to her, not so long ago. "Well done, Becca. Well, done."

Chapter Thirteen

"*Rebecca? Is that you?*"

Rebecca whirled on the heel of her boot, sending dirt and gravel flying. "Where are you, Abi?"

"In the horse barn."

She strode across the yard and stepped into the darkened building. A shaft of light from the window streamed inside, illuminating dust motes dancing wildly in the air along with tiny bits of straw. Evidence that someone had been cleaning stalls.

"Where?"

"Here." Abi popped her head up from a stall and leaned on the rail, pitchfork in hand.

"I've been looking all over for you."

"Sorry, I was bonding with Princess." Her eyes widened as she looked Rebecca up and down. "Aren't you a mess?"

"Me?" Rebecca glanced down at her clothing. "What about you? You've got more straw in your hair than on the ground. And you're covered with dirt."

"Apparently you haven't looked in a mirror lately. There's grease all over your face."

"Of course there is. The lawn mower broke down,

and I've spent the last hour fixing it. I'm now convinced Joe keeps half the equipment around this place running with rubber bands and bubble gum." She looked at Abi. "What's your excuse?"

"Nothing so glamorous here," Abi said as she stepped out of the empty stall and carefully hung the pitchfork on the wall. "Although I can tell you that I've never had so much fun getting dirty."

Rebecca laughed.

"How's the barn look?" Abi waved a hand around her kingdom. "The horses and I are now on a first-name basis."

"You are now a professional mucker. The stalls are beautiful. Even Princess is impressed."

"What's next? Let's not waste time here chatting." Abi snapped her fingers. "There's work to be done."

"Julian says dinner is ready."

Abi pulled her phone out of her pocket and rubbed the screen on her sleeve. "Oh, my, it really is dinnertime. Why, it's been hours since lunch."

"Quite a lunch it was, too."

"Yes. You're right." Abi frowned. "Except that with all those extra hands from Elliott Ranch, you know there weren't any leftovers."

"Did you see their faces?" Rebecca asked. "I think they were stunned. Only Gallagher Ranch brings hot gourmet meals out to the ranch hands in the field."

"They'll be standing in line to work with Joe once the word gets out." Abi yanked off her gloves and tossed them on a stool.

Rebecca nodded. "Julian has totally redeemed himself, don't you think?"

"You've obviously forgotten about your stitches."

"I haven't. Then again, I know what it's like to be crucified for an accident."

"True," Abi said. "You know, I have to admit, this has been a very good couple of days. I am beginning to understand why you like ranch work so much."

"It is satisfying, isn't it? Sunrise to sunset. Nature all around. Man in his element."

"Yes, satisfying until I remember three a.m."

"What do you mean?" Rebecca grabbed two rags from Joe's stack of clean work rags and tossed one to Abi, who began to wipe her face.

"It's sort of like cowgirl Cinderella. Exactly as you said, toiling away, sunrise to sunset. Only she never gets to actually go to the ball. I mean, it really never stops here, does it? Three a.m. always arrives. You keep going and going and going, in perpetuity. At least with my job, I eventually get to type 'The End.'" She turned to Rebecca. "Am I right?"

"On a ranch you bring in the harvest and you take the cows to market."

"That's not exactly what I meant when I said going to the ball."

"I know, which is why ranch life is referred to as a calling. Because it keeps calling you back."

Abi offered a flat laugh. "You can say that again. In fact, you can say it a couple dozen times. I have new respect for Joe Gallagher. For you, too, for that matter. This home-on-the-range life is not for the faint-hearted." She ran her hands through her hair, releasing a flurry of straw.

"Tell me about it. However, it does beat doing paperwork all day long," Rebecca said.

"Are you trying to talk yourself out of your upcoming bonus and promotion?"

"Shh." Once again Rebecca felt the need to glance

around to be certain they weren't overheard. "That is definitely not a done deal."

"Once you deliver the Gallagher goods it is. And they are all but delivered. Do you want to be promoted and work from home, or not?" Abi asked.

"I do. I really do. It means more money and job security. I'm excited at the possibility of staying in Paradise with my family. The thing I hadn't considered is that as a senior case manager I'll have significantly less direct patient care and double the paperwork."

"Maybe you should rethink your career track. It's obvious that you were born to be a rancher. Anyone can see that. Why you're playing around doing anything else is a mystery to me, Rebecca. This is clearly what you're meant to be doing."

"I'd have to have a ranch for that to happen, Abi."

"Like that will be tough. Look around you. Have I mentioned I know a rancher?" Abi stomped her feet, knocking off as much debris as possible. "Come on. We can decide what we want to be when we grow up, later. I want food."

As they walked out, Joe and Rod met them in the yard. Joe stopped walking and his eyes rounded as he assessed first Abi and then Rebecca, his gaze taking in their disheveled and dirty clothes.

Rod sniffed the air. "Ewww. Which one of you two smells like eau de horse? No offense ladies, but you can't come to the table smelling like that."

"It's me, and I'm proud of it," Abi said. "You know, someone has to do the dirty work around here while you guys are out there with those other macho men, playing on those funny looking tractor thingies and that fancy Old MacDonald Bobcat."

"Hey, I resemble that remark," Rod said with a grin.

"Did you see me on that baler? The good news is, we can consider the hay officially harvested."

"Really?" Rebecca looked to Joe for confirmation.

Joe took off his hat and wiped the sweat from his forehead with a cotton bandanna. "Yeah. Never could have done it this fast without Rod's help. Hollis Elliott's guys went to town, as well. I can finish pulling the bales off the field tomorrow. But you folks may consider yourself done."

Abi and Rod offered up a loud cheer and exchanged high fives.

"That's great, isn't it?" Rebecca asked Joe.

"Yeah. For sure." Joe twitched his nose and sneezed. "Abi, I'm going to need you to stand ten paces back."

"I get the hint," Abi said.

"That wasn't exactly a hint," Rod said. "Come on. There's a hose over there. I'll hose down your boots."

"Okay, but let's hurry. My stomach is rumbling," Abi said, racing ahead.

Rebecca smiled and fell into step beside Joe as they walked toward the cottage where Julian had dinner waiting.

"Things have worked out well, haven't they?" she asked him.

"They have, and you never even said 'I told you so.'"

"I'm not an 'I told you so' kind of gal," Rebecca replied.

They walked around Rod's rental SUV, her Honda and the farm truck to cross the gravel drive. As they approached the little house, Rebecca looked up and stopped in her tracks.

The large terra-cotta pots in front of the cottage overflowed with tall crimson geraniums. The deep green foliage was ripe with buds.

"What's this? Who planted the pots?" she asked, turning to Joe.

"Technically, Julian did."

"Technically?"

"He needed something to do between meals, and I sure wasn't going to let him loose on the ranch. I sent him to town for flowers and potting soil. He planted some on the back porch, too." Joe nodded as he examined the pots. "Did a nice job, didn't he?"

"Why would you have him plant flowers?"

"Maybe I like flowers."

"Do you?"

"I'm not opposed to them. Truth is, they're for you. I know you've been too busy to plant and I...well, I wanted to say thank you."

"For what? My time here has been a comedy of errors."

"That's not true."

"Excuse me, but as I recall, it was so bad that you kicked us off the ranch last week." She chuckled.

"That may have been a knee-jerk reaction on my part."

Rebecca smiled. "That's one way to look at it."

He cleared his throat and glanced at her and then away. "Becca?"

"Yes?"

"I am indebted to you for talking to Mr. Elliott. You saved the day." He offered a sheepish smile. "I know I talk a good game, but you recognized that I really needed assistance even though I didn't want to admit it. Thank you."

"You're very welcome. Glad I could help."

Rebecca knelt to examine the flowers. Stroking a velvet petal with a finger, she took a deep breath. "I'm not going to be here long enough to enjoy these blooms."

"Is there a rush? You said you have more certification stuff to check off."

"Just that paperwork you've avoided and the manufacturer DVD. We've covered everything else." She looked up at him. "Except for your grumbling, you've been an exemplary patient. A quick study, as well. Just as you promised you would be."

"Maybe we could talk about that."

"Talk about what? Your grumbling?"

"No. For that I can only apologize."

"Apology accepted."

Joe nodded. "Look Becca, we've come a long way, don't you think? I mean, well, it seems to me that things have changed lately. Gotten back to where we can trust each other again." He looked at the ground before slowly, hesitantly, meeting her gaze.

"I hope so, Joe." She rubbed her arm, a nervous gesture she still hadn't overcome.

"How's the incision?" he asked.

She pushed up her sleeve and let him see the clean line of stitches. "They're healing nicely. I've got an appointment to have the sutures removed tomorrow."

When Joe gently wrapped his fingers around her wrist to examine the wound, she stilled at his touch.

"It's healing." He met her gaze, his eyes tender with emotion. "Like you and me. We've reconciled the past. Maybe it's time to talk about where we go from here." His words were a soft murmur.

"Oh?" Rebecca swallowed.

The front door burst open and Julian stood on the porch, hands on hips and a spatula in his hand. "The boeuf bourguignon is getting cold, people."

"We'll talk later," he said, releasing her arm.

Rebecca nodded and followed him up the steps to the cottage.

Something she hadn't felt in a long time began to bubble up inside her. Hope. Had Joe truly forgiven her for the past? *Did she dare to hope that he wanted to consider the future?*

The sound of voices drifted to Joe as he passed by the side of the cottage on his way home after evening chores were completed. Though he knew he shouldn't, he slowed his steps. Nothing good ever came from eavesdropping, yet he couldn't help himself. He grinned. He'd blame his mother. It was no doubt genetic.

"So what do you think, Abi?" Julian's voice rang out.

"What are you babbling on about, Julian?"

"He's waxing philosophical now that he's headed back to the big city," Rod said. "He's been doing it since he served dessert tonight."

"What do you think about Paradise and this ranch life?" Julian continued, ignoring Rod's jab.

"That's a no-brainer. Paradise is a wonderful town. This ranch is terrific, and Rebecca is one blessed woman."

"Awe, come on, Abi. That's a little over the top. Especially for you. I count on you to be a realist," Julian returned.

"I am being a realist."

"Okay, then maybe you can shed some insight into what's going on with Rebecca and Joe."

"That's none of our business," she said.

"Oh, you're no fun. We're just talking."

"Gossiping is more like it."

"Whatever."

Joe could envision Julian shrugging his bony shoulders about now.

"I'm simply speculating. Do you think Rebecca's going to give up everything for a cowboy who runs a little ranch in the middle of Nowhereville?"

"That's none of our business, either," Abi retorted. "But for the record, Nowhereville is her hometown, and she and the cowboy have history. Personally, I'd take that package if it was offered to me."

"I was wondering about that myself, Abi," Rod chimed in. "She's got a chunk of change coming to her for this project. Do you think she's planning to stay in Paradise or go back to Denver?"

"You aren't supposed to know about the bonus," Abi snapped.

"It's common grapevine knowledge," Rod said. "If she brings the completed Joe Gallagher assignment to OrthoBorne on deadline, she's got a promotion and a mega-huge bonus in her pocket."

Joe swallowed, trying to digest what he was hearing.

Rod continued. "I can't believe Julian nearly blew it for her."

"What? You've never messed up before?" Julian asked, indignation in his voice.

"Plenty of times. But Rebecca has a twelve-inch souvenir down her arm thanks to you," Rod returned.

"It was an accident. What else can I do to make it up to her?"

"Stay out of trouble."

"Only twelve more hours, Julian," Abi warned. "And I agree, Rod. Rebecca deserves whatever she earned on this project."

"We haven't ever talked about it," Rod said. "But it's no secret that she's had a rough couple of years. She really deserves a chance to start over."

"Is that fresh off the grapevine, too?" Abi asked.

"*Denver Post*, Abi. I read the paper. Everyone in the office is aware. How could they not be?"

"Still, it's not right for us to talk about Rebecca when she's not here. Who has the keys? I suggest we head for town to pack up our stuff. We leave early tomorrow."

"Hey, I didn't mean anything by it. You know I care about Rebecca, the same as you," Rod said.

"I know." She sighed. "I just feel bad. She's a good person, and she deserves the best."

"Absolutely," Rod said.

"The best," Joe whispered as he shoved off the wall, his gut burning. Yeah, Becca deserved the best. He changed direction and walked behind the cottage and through the trees to the corral so as not to be seen.

The sound of a car starting indicated that the OrthoBorne group was indeed headed back to town.

Joe slammed the palm of his left hand against the top rail of the corral, causing the entire fence to vibrate. He'd nearly made a fool of himself. Again. Nearly put his heart on the line for the second time with this woman.

Hadn't he learned anything in twelve years? The first time he was a naive kid. At thirty-three, he should know better. He'd let down his defenses only to discover that Becca was stringing him along until she had a grasp on something better.

Joe Gallagher was an assignment. A means to an end. Nothing more.

He stared out at the slow-setting pink of sunset. Had she really been playing him all along?

"Joe?" Becca's cheerful voice called out.

He stiffened but didn't turn, willing himself to stay strong. One glance at her and his resolve would be shot to pieces.

"Did you want to talk?" She slid a booted foot on the bottom rail and relaxed her arms over the top one.

"No. I'm headed to the house. I've got to get up early and get those bales off the field in case it decides to rain."

"I'll help."

"That's not necessary. This is my job, and I can do it, thanks to you and OrthoBorne."

"Are you sure? I can ride the tractor while you—"

Joe held up a hand. "Becca, you're here to get me certified. It's never been part of your job description to be a ranch hand."

He refused to meet her gaze.

"I like working on the ranch," she said.

"Sure you do."

"What's that supposed to mean?" Annoyance now laced her voice.

He feigned interest in the sunset. Overhead the halogen lights, set on timers, sizzled to life.

"It means you've been very flexible. You've gone above and beyond to get this project completed. I'm very appreciative. Gallagher Ranch is appreciative. But your job is done."

"Terrific. Back to doing it all by yourself, I see. Good for you, Mr. Gallagher."

He clenched his jaw and struggled for control. "Look, I'm saying thank you. Everything has gone according to plan. The team has completed its assignment, the hay is harvested and you can tell OrthoBorne that you brought Joe Gallagher in on schedule."

He heard her soft gasp.

Silence stretched between them. In the barn a horse whinnied.

"Your certification?" she asked.

"I'll have that paperwork all filled out by morning. I can watch the DVD tonight."

"All right," she murmured.

He held up his myoelectric arm toward the sky and offered a bitter laugh. "I'm paid for. Doesn't get any better than that, does it?"

"No, I guess not."

He heard her footfalls on the dirt and gravel as she turned away. Then she stopped. "Have I done something wrong?" The softly spoken question drifted to him.

"Not a thing." Joe swallowed, determined to see this through. "You can hide the key under the mat when you leave. No rush. But I know you have things to do. Places to be."

Now Joe did turn from the fence. Becca's face was void of emotion. She stared through him for a moment, out into the deep darkness, before she turned and walked toward the house, her back ramrod straight.

Maybe if she stayed their paths would cross in town, then and again, but that was all. They'd go back to being strangers.

Julian was right. Becca deserved more than this little ranch in Nowhereville, which was about all he could ever hope to offer her.

Funny thing was when he really thought about it, he didn't blame her. She had a child to consider this time around. It didn't seem necessary to do much praying on the matter. No, it was clear that once again this cowboy bit the dust.

He'd dismissed her.

Rebecca barely resisted slamming the door of the cottage. She paced the floor, grateful Casey was at her grandmother's. Mind made up, she headed to the laundry-room closet where cardboard boxes had been carefully broken down and stored. Yanking them out, Rebecca grabbed the packing tape from the shelf and savagely ripped strips of tape from the dispenser, slapping them on the boxes. When one was put together, she tossed it into the hall and started on another.

Energized by her anger, she began to shove laundry supplies into the same boxes, then sealed them with more tape.

Like an out of control tornado, releasing years of anger she moved to the kitchen. Slamming pots and pans, she tossed them into boxes, as well.

How dare he? How dare Joe Gallagher shut her out?

Opening another cupboard, her gaze landed on the refrigerator where a souvenir from the Fourth of July barbecue at Elliott Ranch was held in place by a flower magnet.

A photo of Casey and Joe. What would she tell her little girl? Casey had fallen in love with Joe, just like her momma.

Rebecca hitched a breath and a sob escaped.

Her knees buckled, and she slid against the cupboards down to the floor. Closing her eyes, she fought the tears that threatened.

"No. I am not going to cry." She swiped at her face with the back of her hand and then sat up straight, stirring up as much anger and indignation as she could muster. "No crying. I've come too far. I've endured much worse than this. I will not waste my tears on Joe Gallagher."

She licked away a drop of moisture from her lips.

How had this happened? This was a job. An assignment. A bunch of ordinary manila folders with patient-care plans. Assessment, intervention and goals. Period. It wasn't supposed to get personal.

Falling in love with Joe Gallagher hadn't been part of the plan.

Rebecca covered her face with her hands and allowed her shoulders to sag under the weight of her despair.

She hadn't imagined things, had she? They were growing closer and closer.

So what had changed? What did she do wrong? Whatever it was, the walls were up and Joe wasn't going to talk.

And figuring it out wasn't her priority. She had a daughter to think of. Casey was what really mattered.

Besides, if she'd learned one thing in the last few years, it was that Virginia was right. Fixing other people wasn't her responsibility. She wasn't to blame for someone else's issues.

She could train Joe in the use of his myoelectric arm, but she couldn't fix what was going on inside the cowboy.

Chapter Fourteen

Joe stood in the yard with the dogs at his heels. For the fifth or sixth time today, he'd forgotten what he was about to do next. His thinking had been muddled since the day began.

He blamed it on a sleepless night. Now he simply couldn't focus. Animals fed. Check. Hay bales in from the field. Check. Those chores had taken up the bulk of his morning. Maybe he'd just clean off the equipment and call it a day.

Overhead the clouds moved quickly and the sky had begun to darken ominously. Eighty percent chance of rain tonight. Like he trusted the weather guy anymore. Rain would be here long before tonight.

Across the yard he could see the cottage. The Honda was absent from its usual spot. Becca had probably gone into town. He'd promised to drop off the paperwork and DVD. May as well do that now before that slipped his mind, too. Joe strode into the barn, picked up the packet from the counter and headed across the yard.

With every plodding step toward the geranium-filled pots, he once again began to second-guess the decision he'd made last night. Had he done the right thing?

Sure he had. It was time, once and for all, to bury the past. Joe dug in his pocket and pulled out the ring box he'd retrieved from his drawer this morning. Twelve years he'd been holding on to this dream.

Time to let it go. He'd bury this ring—literally—and finally lay his past to rest.

Alone on his land once more. Wasn't that what he wanted? A future he could control. Everything to return to normal?

He knocked several times first, then using his key to open the cottage door, he stepped inside and froze, stunned at the sight of neat stacks of sealed packing boxes in the entryway, all labeled with Becca's precise handwriting. Kitchen. Bath. Casey's room.

Becca hadn't wasted any time.

Joe walked slowly through the house, his boots echoing on the hardwood floors. The beds had been stripped. He paused in the doorway of Casey's pink bedroom. The room was empty, the blinds sadly drawn, blocking the view of the ranch.

Every single trace of Becca and Casey had been scrubbed and polished from the cottage. The place sparkled. Floors had been mopped, the windows cleaned.

It looked better than when she'd moved in.

He paused and ran a hand over his jaw. No. He apparently hadn't made the wrong decision. She knew it, too. Once again, Becca had wiped herself from his life, as though she'd never existed.

Yeah, it was time for him to do the same. Joe tossed the packet and DVD on the counter.

He closed the front door and stood on the porch. Before he realized what he was doing, he kicked over a pot of geraniums with his boot, his frustration bubbling over.

Around him a cleansing rain began to fall. Tucking

his myoelectric prosthesis safely beneath his coat to keep
the expensive device safe from the moisture, he stepped
off the porch and started walking.

And he kept on walking. Right out of Rebecca's life.

"I thought we were going to miss saying goodbye to
you," Abi said as she hugged Rebecca.

"Sorry. The doctor's appointment took longer than
expected."

"That's okay. We stocked up on Patti Jo's finest while
we waited," Rod said with a laugh. "Though no doubt
we're going to be going through Patti Jo withdrawal before the week is out."

The SUV had been conveniently parked outside the
bakery, where Rebecca had pulled up only moments before in her Honda.

While Rod and Julian rearranged the equipment and
luggage, Abi grabbed Rebecca's arm and pulled her to
the curb.

"Are you all right?" she asked. "You look awful."

"I'm fine. Never better." Rebecca plastered on a jaunty
smile. "A little insomnia."

"What's going on?" Abi demanded.

"Nothing."

"That might work with someone else, but not with
me." Abi crossed her arms and stood waiting.

"Joe," Rebecca finally admitted on a hushed whisper.
"Last night. He told me he was ready for me to leave Gallagher Ranch."

"Oh, Rebecca. And you believed him?"

"Of course I did. I was awake all night replaying his
words over and over. He shut me out. I can't fight that.
Besides, the way I see it, it's better to hurt now than to

realize later that I'm making a terrible mistake. I've spent the last twelve years down that road."

Abi frowned and looked her up and down. "I never would have taken you for a quitter."

Rebecca jerked to attention at the words. "I'm not a quitter."

"Then get back to that ranch and fight for what you want. I mean it." Abi nodded. "And remember, you have my number. If you need someone to talk to, call me."

"I will. I will," Rebecca promised as she considered her friend's words. Overwhelmed, she reached out to embrace Abi in a bear hug.

"Excuse me," Julian interrupted, offering Rebecca an air kiss. "I need some love, too."

"Look at this, Julian," Rebecca said. She held out her arm, no longer ashamed of the other ugly scar. "The stitches were removed today."

"I'm so relieved," he said. "All is forgiven then?"

"Yes," Rebecca said.

"Okay," Rod said. "We've got to get going. We have things to do and it's starting to rain." Holding a hand in the air to catch the intermittent drops, he glanced up at the sky. "We'll be soaked if we stand here much longer." He looked to Rebecca. "We'll see you sometime soon at the home office, right?"

She nodded.

"Remember what I said," Abi called out from inside the vehicle.

Rebecca smiled and waved at the SUV as it pulled away from the curb. She continued to stare until it disappeared down Main Street. Joe would be glad they were gone, but she would miss them. Especially Abi.

When all was said and done, the team had done a

great job. She'd seen the prints, the video footage and read Abi's interview.

There was no doubt in her mind that she would get the promotion and the bonus.

Which was too bad.

Because she knew in her heart that she'd give it all up for a chance to stay on Gallagher Ranch. But that was silly. Her second chance was gone. No matter what Abi believed.

Joe Gallagher wanted things to go back to the way they were. Well, now he had his wish.

Rebecca got in the Honda and drove slowly back to the ranch, savoring her last drive. Drizzle tap-danced on her windshield, and the wipers sang a rhythmic song. She smiled at the riotous wildflowers in the fields along the route to the ranch as they swayed in the rainy breeze. The blooms stretched across the fields on either side of the road for miles until the tall conifers appeared. The stately pines led the rest of the way to Gallagher Ranch.

All she had to do was stick the boxes in the car and she was done. She'd stay at her mother's until she decided what was next.

By the time she parked outside the cottage the rain had stopped, leaving only muddy puddles in the yard outside the barn and the equipment garage.

In front of the cottage a pot had been overturned. She frowned, kneeling to carefully right the container, scoop the fallen soil back into the pot and pat it back into place around the flowers.

"You'll be just fine," she whispered to the plant.

Shaking the dirt from her hands, she picked up her keys from the ground and opened the front door.

The first thing she saw was the packet and the DVD.

Joe had been here. Rebecca released a loud sigh of frustration.

She grabbed a box and headed to the car, popping open the trunk. Dumping it inside, she glanced around the ranch yard.

It was quiet. Almost too quiet. A shiver slid over her. Something wasn't right.

Rebecca walked to the horse barn. Blackie was in his stall, as was Princess. Gil and Wishbone were in the back of the barn snoozing on their backs.

She'd miss the ranch animals when she was gone. Miss the morning rides with them into the pasture. The smells of sunrise on Gallagher Ranch. Memories rushed in, overwhelming her. She swallowed hard and kept moving.

Pulling open the equipment garage only told her that the farm truck was gone. Joe was out there somewhere. Alone, per his request.

When the squawk of the CB radio rang out into the silence, echoing against the metal walls of the garage, Rebecca jumped.

"Joe Gallagher. Need help..."

The radio sizzled and crackled, cutting off his words. She waited for moments, hoping for more. Finally, she picked up the radio's receiver and depressed the button on the device as she spoke. "Joe. Message received. This is Rebecca. Come in, Joe."

She waited again, but there was no response.

"Where are you, Joe?"

Nothing. Was she the only one who'd heard him? Should she call Sam? She tamped down panic, instead formulating a plan.

It would be faster to check the ranch herself. In the last weeks, she'd memorized nearly every inch of the land.

Rebecca ran straight for the barn. She approached the

chestnut mare's stall, and then hesitated. Yes, she'd been cleared to ride by the doctor, but was she ready, after the way Princess had tossed her?

Her stomach didn't think so. It didn't matter. She had no choice.

"Are we ready, Princess?" she whispered in soothing tones to the horse, as she stroked her mane. "We have to be. Joe needs us."

Rebecca put on a rain slicker and quickly tacked up the horse. She whistled for Gil and Wishbone. The dogs rallied to her, running in eager circles, ready for action. She mounted and rode out across the yard to the pasture.

Did they get any sorrier than him?

Joe sat on a boulder massaging his ankle. He'd driven out to the far corner of the ranch and broke an axle in a shallow water-filled creek, which he would have seen if he'd been paying attention and not thinking about Becca as he drove through the sudden downpour. Sure, he could blame it on the rain, but he and God both knew it was his own fault.

Overhead a hawk soared, making circles, as though the bird was examining Joe's predicament and no doubt laughing.

Yeah, he was alone on his ranch. Things were back to normal, exactly the way he'd claimed for weeks that he wanted them to be. Now he had all the time in the world to ponder his words which were coming back to haunt him.

Where was Becca now? Come evening, if not sooner, she would be long gone. She was never coming back.

He'd accused his brother of being foolish for not going after the love of his life, and lo and behold, the woman loved him so much she'd come back.

Happily-ever-after for Dan.

Not so much for him.

No. Joe Gallagher had to learn everything the hard way.

He'd lost the only woman he'd ever loved.

Twice.

Even he had to admit that was quite pathetic.

Yeah, he was in a fine fix all the way around. The truck was out of commission, and he'd twisted his ankle crawling out the passenger door after it'd ended up sideways in the creek bed. To make things even more fun, his phone was dead because he'd forgotten to charge it, and the CB had gotten wet, offering him little more than a snap, crackle and pop when he turned on the thing.

Joe was more than aggravated. He shoved his Stetson to the back of his head, grateful that while he'd lost his dignity, he still had his hat.

A glance at his watch reminded him that he'd been out here two hours now. He'd finished off the water and the granola bar in his jacket pocket an hour ago. He was damp and tired. His ankle hurt.

It was going to get cold real soon, too. There was only a few more hours of daylight. Yeah, he was turning into a pitiful excuse for a cowboy.

He rubbed his hands over his face and started to pray. Hopefully the good Lord wasn't laughing so hard at how he'd messed up his life that He would miss the prayer that was just sent up. After all, He wasn't used to hearing from Joe so often. He might not even recognize his voice.

The pounding of hooves on the land filled the silence, becoming louder and louder. Joe's head snapped up at the sound. A horse and rider appeared in the distance. Silhouetted against the dark clouds on the horizon, a woman in a taupe Stetson approached at a rapid clip, with two dogs racing alongside.

Becca?

When she was inches from him, she stopped, reined in Princess and stared down at him, shaking her head but saying nothing.

"What are you doing out here?" he asked. "You aren't even supposed to be on a horse."

"I can go back if you want." She clucked her tongue and lifted the reins.

"No. No. Wait. I'm sorry."

"Finally we agree on something," she muttered.

He frowned.

"I've been cleared to ride. I went to the doctor this morning."

"Good. That's good." His heart began to beat funny in his chest as he stared up at her on Princess. She looked good. Real good. More important, she hadn't left the ranch.

Becca glanced around, her eyes rounding when she turned in the saddle and saw the truck. "What happened?"

"I had a little accident."

"Good thing you have backup, huh?"

He narrowed his eyes. That was as close as she'd probably ever come to an 'I told you so'—however, he was in no position to point out the obvious.

"How did you find me?"

"The CB radio. All I could get was that you needed help."

"Yeah, but how did you know where to find me?"

"I didn't. I prayed and rode the fence line. Gil and Wishbone told me you were here."

Hearing their names mentioned, the dogs began to bark and run in circles around Princess.

"Sit," Becca commanded. The dogs immediately obeyed. She looked back over at the creek. "What did you do to the truck?"

Joe glanced away. "That's a long story."

"No bars on your cell?"

"Forgot to plug it in last night." He stood and grimaced as he balanced on one boot.

"Are you okay?"

"I twisted my right ankle. It's not broken or anything. Just needs a little ice and I'll be fine."

"Sure you will. Maybe I should call an ambulance."

"Not funny."

She shrugged, unsmiling. "I thought it was really amusing."

"You mind if we ride double back to the ranch?"

Becca slid off Princess and led the horse close to him. "I mind and so does Princess. You ride and I'll walk."

"No way. I'm not doing that."

"Take it or leave it, Gallagher."

This time it was his eyes that rounded. "You drive a mighty hard bargain."

"Oh, you have no idea. Do you want help getting on the horse?"

"I can manage."

"Of course you can."

She held Princess steady as he hobbled over and ungracefully dumped himself into the saddle.

Becca was silent as they walked for the next thirty minutes. When they got close to the barn, she stopped.

"What do you want to do?" she asked.

"Let's get Princess taken care of first. Then if you could help me up to the house, I can handle things from there." He glanced over at the Honda. "You've already got it packed up."

"Only just started, but it turns out I don't have as much stuff as I thought. My baggage seems to thin down every day."

"What about Casey?" Joe asked.

Becca turned her face away, revealing nothing. "No big deal. She has a room at my mom's, too."

"But she likes this one. It's pink."

"Joe, I'm done here. Let's not get all morbid. You had your say yesterday. Besides, the truth is you really didn't need much help from me to start. A much-deserved kick in the pants, maybe, but that was about it."

"Hey, no need to be insulting," he said as he rode into the barn. He slid down from Princess, grimacing as he landed. Grabbing the top stall rail, he propped his boot on the rung. "So you got your bonus and the promotion. What's next?"

Becca stared at him. Her jaw sagged slightly, and she released a small gasp. "Is that what this is all about?" She didn't wait for an answer. "Who told you about the bonus and promotion?"

He shrugged.

Becca paced across the barn. "Seriously, you never even bothered to ask me?"

"What's to ask? You did a great job and now you're done."

"Yes. That's right. I got that bonus for doing my job. So what? It doesn't change anything. It wasn't even my idea. As for the promotion, it means I get to stay in Paradise, and that is everything to me."

She turned and met his gaze. "We had a second chance, Joe. Except you insist on living your so-called back-to-normal life here all by yourself."

Joe inhaled sharply at the words he himself had been thinking just a short while ago.

"I can't make you ask for help, Joe. I can't make you reach out to me. That's what cuts deep." Once again she paced back and forth. "I get that other-shoe-dropping mentality. I used to sing the exact same song when I arrived at the ranch. But haven't I proved you can trust me?"

"It wasn't about you."

"What does that even mean, Joe?"

"It means that I'm terrified you'll find out you don't really want to be here. On a ranch in the middle of nowhere with a handicapped man. I'm scared I'll let down my guard, and you'll decide you want to be with someone who can give you what you really deserve. It's been twelve years, Becca, and I still can't offer you anything but hay, cows and a house in the middle of nowhere."

"So basically you turned me away to save yourself?"

Joe sighed. "Yeah, when you put it that way, it does sound pretty sorry."

"If you hadn't dumped that truck, I would have been out of here. Long gone. We're both so pigheaded and afraid, that we're missing out on what's right in front of us."

She walked up to him, getting smack-dab in the middle of his personal space.

"Do you love me, Joe Gallagher?"

He took a deep breath. "I keep telling myself that you don't fall in love with someone in three weeks. But my heart says that you do if you've been in love with her all your life."

Her eyes widened.

Joe neatly wrapped his arms around her. His left arm was gently around her waist, capturing her close, and his prosthesis rested on her hip, assuring her he would never let her fall.

Becca put her hand up to gently touch his cheek.

"I also need you to have faith in yourself, Joe. Otherwise you'll never have faith in us."

He closed his eyes and then opened them. She was still there, as beautiful as ever. She met his gaze, unwavering.

"I'm sorry, Becca. I'm sorry. I do believe in us. I was afraid."

She smiled, and her hand caressed his face.

Joe tipped his hat back with a finger, and the Stetson rolled off his head onto the floor. Didn't matter. Cowboys couldn't kiss properly with their hats on. Everyone knew that.

"Careful with your foot. Don't fall," she murmured.

"I got this covered."

His head lowered inch by inch until his lips rested on hers. Becca's hat fell to the ground as he closed his eyes and kissed the love of his life over and over again.

"Oh, Joe," she murmured. Looking slightly dazed, she held on to his biceps. "What are we going to do now?"

"Becca, do you love me?"

"I love you, Joe Gallagher."

"Seems pretty simple to me. Let me show you something." He pulled the ring box out of a pocket of his Levi's and handed it to her.

"What is this?"

"It's the ring I bought for you twelve years ago."

Her eyes welled with moisture, and she licked her lips. "I've wasted so much time. I've made so many wrong decisions."

"Stop that. This is all about us. We're right where we're supposed to be, right now."

Becca opened the box and stared at the marquis-cut diamond. She released a small gasp. "It's beautiful."

"Not real big."

"I said it's beautiful. The prettiest thing I've ever seen." She looked up at him. "What did you plan to do with this ring?"

He swallowed. "There is only one thing I ever wanted to do with this ring. Becca, will you marry me?"

"Yes," she breathed softly.

Joe's own breath caught, his chest swelling with happiness when he saw the love in her eyes.

Becca held out her hand and he slipped the diamond on her finger.

"What do you think? Should I exchange it?"

Becca splayed her fingers against his heart and examined the ring on her hand.

"Never." She smiled. "It's perfect."

Joe reached down and lifted her fingers using his prosthetic hand. He kissed each of them tenderly.

"I love you, Joe."

He sighed. "I love you, too, Becca. Forever."

Epilogue

Joe slid off Blackie and plucked a stalk of sweet grass from the ground and bit into it. First signs of spring. Clover and orchard grass were starting to come up in the pasture, as well. Raising his face to the sky, he inhaled.

Yes. Rain was on the way. That was okay. Better than snow. The long winter had finally passed. Now it was the time of renewal and rebirth for the land.

Behind him a horse whinnied. Gil and Wishbone barked a vigorous note of welcome, turning in eager circles. Joe turned, as well. Where was Mushy? He whistled, and the new pup came running from under a bush, with his black-and-white tail dancing as he ran.

Joe looked up in time to see a horse and rider approach.

Becca. His wife.

"How's the Gallagher Ranch foreman today?" Joe asked.

"Good." She glanced at the sky. "It's going to rain." Becca shuddered.

"What's the matter?" he asked?"

"I smell manure, and it's about to make me gag."

"I guess your smeller is working."

"In spades."

He gazed up at her, realizing once again what a blessed man he was. "I thought you were in town."

"I was. Oh, and that tractor part won't be in for another week. I stopped by to check for you."

"That's not good. How am I supposed to till your garden without the tractor?"

"It will wait another week. It's not like we don't have plenty to do around here."

"You're right," he agreed. "And we did promise the church they could have their Easter sunrise service out here on the ranch this year. Getting ready for that will keep us running."

Joe cocked his head. He was missing something here, and he wasn't sure what. Then it hit him. "Didn't you have a doctor's appointment?"

"I did."

"Everything okay?"

"More than okay." A smile lit up her face.

"What could be more than okay?"

"We're having a baby."

Joe nearly swallowed the blade of grass in his mouth. "A baby?" He almost choked.

"Well, if you want to get technical, we're having two babies."

This time he did choke.

Becca slid from her mare and came over to slap him on the back. "Are you okay?"

"When were you going to tell me about two babies?"

"I was thinking up all sorts of ways to surprise you. But then you asked." She shrugged. "I have a hard time keeping secrets."

"Twins?"

"You can blame your mother for that one. They run in your family, not mine."

"When?" he sputtered.

"You know these things take nine months. There's only ten or twenty days difference in the gestation period between my babies and your cows. Your cattle and I may be giving birth right around the same time."

"You don't say?" Joe stood there stunned for a moment, then he swiftly moved to cover her lips with his own.

"Mmm, that was nice," Becca murmured.

"I love you, Becca. Have I said that enough lately?"

"I love you, too, and you can never say it enough." She paused. "I'm thinking it's going to be boys."

"What? Did the doctor tell you that?"

"No. I've just got this gut feeling. The doctor said they can confirm in a few weeks." Becca punctuated the words with another quick kiss. "What do you think about Joseph and Jackson?"

Joe laughed. "What if it's girls? My sisters are twins."

"I'm telling you. It's boys."

"You're not even going to consider girls?"

"I like baby girls as much as the next momma, but my babies are little boys."

"I'm thinking it might be time to take that parcel of land that Hollis Elliott has been begging me for and finally build my big house."

"So he was right?"

"Who?"

"Hollis. He told me you'd never sell that land. You were bluffing me."

"Apparently so. I'd do anything to keep you here at Gallagher Ranch. You should know that by now."

She shook her head.

"I may need to hire a new foreman, as well. Too bad, I was nearly finished breaking in the new one. And I really like her."

"Not so fast. I'm not retiring for quite some time. Eight more months, to be exact."

"How long can you keep riding a horse?"

"The doctor said that as long as I feel safe, he'd approve walking my horse until my third month."

"Not really?"

"Yes. However, after some prayer, I've decided that I'm really making decisions for the three of us. Joseph Jr., Jackson and me. So today will be my last ride until after the babies are born. You can buy me a new all-terrain vehicle instead of a horse."

He rubbed a hand over his face and grabbed a water bottle from his saddlebag.

"Joe, are you all right?"

"Not really. I'm still pretty much flabbergasted. How'd I get so blessed?"

"By keeping your eyes on Him."

"Do you think Casey will be okay with this?"

"Are you kidding? More than okay. She's been green-eyed ever since Amy told her Dan and Beth are having a baby."

"Wow, our boys and Dan's son will grow up together."

"The Gallagher tradition marches on." Becca sighed. "Thank you, Joe."

"For what? Aside from the obvious, I think it's pretty clear I didn't do much, yet I've never been so happy. Why, when I go to town I can hardly get anything accomplished for people asking me why I'm smiling."

Becca laughed. "You've done plenty. You gave me a second chance in Paradise." She reached up and put her arms around his neck and whispered against his mouth. "Thank you, cowboy."

* * * * *

If you loved this story,
pick up these heartwarming books
from beloved author Tina Radcliffe:

THE RANCHER'S REUNION
OKLAHOMA REUNION
MENDING THE DOCTOR'S HEART
STRANDED WITH THE RANCHER
SAFE IN THE FIREMAN'S ARMS
ROCKY MOUNTAIN REUNION

Available now from Love Inspired!

Find more great reads at www.LoveInspired.com

Dear Reader,

Thank you for coming along with me on another journey to Paradise, Colorado. Paradise is a fictional town set in the vicinity of Del Norte, Colorado, west of Denver.

I have to admit that I fell a little bit in love with Joe Gallagher when he appeared in his brother Dan Gallagher's book, *Stranded in Paradise*. I knew then that he had a story to tell, and that he deserved a very special heroine. Rebecca is that woman.

Rebecca and Joe learn, as we must, that looking forward when the events of our past are painful, and even tragic, is never easy. This story holds the familiar threads of forgiveness. Forgiving ourselves, and others. When we are obedient to forgive, eventually the past becomes simply a story that is told, and somehow the Lord enables us to move forward unencumbered by those things that would hold us prisoner. He also provides a future that unfolds in wonderful ways we never could have imagined. Thank You, Lord!

Drop me a line and let me know what you think about this story. I can be reached at tina@tinaradcliffe.com.

Thank you so much.
Tina Radcliffe

REQUEST YOUR FREE BOOKS!

2 FREE INSPIRATIONAL NOVELS
PLUS 2
FREE
MYSTERY GIFTS

YES! Please send me 2 FREE Love Inspired® novels and my 2 FREE mystery gifts (gifts are worth about $10). After receiving them, if I don't wish to receive any more books, I can return the shipping statement marked "cancel." If I don't cancel, I will receive 6 brand-new novels every month and be billed just $4.99 per book in the U.S. or $5.49 per book in Canada. That's a saving of at least 17% off the cover price. It's quite a bargain! Shipping and handling is just 50¢ per book in the U.S. and 75¢ per book in Canada.* I understand that accepting the 2 free books and gifts places me under no obligation to buy anything. I can always return a shipment and cancel at any time. Even if I never buy another book, the two free books and gifts are mine to keep forever.

105/305 IDN GH5P

Name _____ (PLEASE PRINT)

Address _____ Apt. #

City _____ State/Prov. _____ Zip/Postal Code

Signature (if under 18, a parent or guardian must sign)

Mail to the Reader Service:
IN U.S.A.: P.O. Box 1867, Buffalo, NY 14240-1867
IN CANADA: P.O. Box 609, Fort Erie, Ontario L2A 5X3

**Are you a subscriber to Love Inspired® books
and want to receive the larger-print edition?
Call 1-800-873-8635 or visit www.ReaderService.com.**

* Terms and prices subject to change without notice. Prices do not include applicable taxes. Sales tax applicable in N.Y. Canadian residents will be charged applicable taxes. Offer not valid in Quebec. This offer is limited to one order per household. Not valid for current subscribers to Love Inspired books. All orders subject to credit approval. Credit or debit balances in a customer's account(s) may be offset by any other outstanding balance owed by or to the customer. Please allow 4 to 6 weeks for delivery. Offer available while quantities last.

Your Privacy—The Reader Service is committed to protecting your privacy. Our Privacy Policy is available online at www.ReaderService.com or upon request from the Reader Service.

We make a portion of our mailing list available to reputable third parties that offer products we believe may interest you. If you prefer that we not exchange your name with third parties, or if you wish to clarify or modify your communication preferences, please visit us at www.ReaderService.com/consumerschoice or write to us at Reader Service Preference Service, P.O. Box 9062, Buffalo, NY 14240-9062. Include your complete name and address.

LI15

Wyatt glanced at Carolina, but she wouldn't meet his
eyes.

Was she feeling guilty over all Matty's firsts that she'd
denied Wyatt? First breath, first word, the first step Matty
took?

He couldn't say he felt sorry for her. She should be
feeling guilty. She'd made the decision to walk away.
She'd created these consequences for herself, and for
Wyatt, and most of all, for Matty.

But today wasn't a day for anger. Today was about
spending time with his son.

"What do you say, little man?" he asked, scooping
Matty into his arms and leading Carolina to his truck.
"Do you want to play ball?"

Not knowing what Matty would like, he'd pretty
much loaded up every kind of sports ball imaginable—a
football, a baseball, a soccer ball and a basketball.

Carolina flashed him half a smile and shrugged
apologetically. "I'm afraid I don't know much about

these games beyond being able to identify which ball goes with which sport."

"That's what Matty's got a dad for."

He didn't really think about what he was saying until the words had already left his lips.

Their gazes met and locked. She was silently challenging him, but he didn't know about what. Still, he kept his gaze firmly on hers. His words might not have been premeditated, but that didn't make them any less true. He was sorry if he'd hurt her feelings, though. He wanted to keep things friendly between them.

"There's plenty of room on the green for three. What do you say? Do you want to play soccer with us?"

Shock registered in her face, but it was no more than what he was feeling. This was all so new. Untested waters.

Somehow, they had to work things out, but kicking a ball around together at the park?

Why, that almost felt as if they were a family.

And although in a sense that was technically true, Wyatt didn't even want to go down that road.

He had every intention of being the best father he could to Matty. And in so doing, he would establish some sort of a working relationship with Carolina, some way they could both be comfortable without it getting awkward. He just couldn't bring himself to think about that right now.

Or maybe he just didn't want to.

Don't miss
THE DOCTOR'S TEXAS BABY
by Deb Kastner, available February 2017
wherever Love Inspired® books and ebooks are sold.

www.LoveInspired.com

LIEXP0117

Turn your love of reading into
rewards you'll love with
Harlequin My Rewards

**Join for FREE today at
www.HarlequinMyRewards.com**

Earn **FREE BOOKS** of your choice.

Experience **EXCLUSIVE OFFERS** and contests.

Enjoy **BOOK RECOMMENDATIONS**
selected just for you.

PLUS! Sign up now
and get **500** points
right away!

Earn
FREE
REWARDS
HarlequinMyRewards.com
Join
Today!

MYR16R